Deer Run

Deer Run

EDWARD CONNOLLY

Charles Scribner's Sons
New York

To my daughter, Cressida

Chapter One

For every mile of paved highway there were fifty miles of dirt roads. Josh could have wandered aimlessly across the state for months inquiring at gas stations and dilapidated antique shops, or he might have taken a map and chosen arbitrarily any village or township in Vermont. Instead, he remembered a small, trim village that he had passed through as a child while on a tour of historic New England. He remembered how he had lain in the back seat, made sleepy and slightly ill by the dry, dusty air from the car heater that his grandparents required. He remembered how he had glanced up and seen the name Heartwell on a small wooden sign, how he had been fascinated by the whiteness of the town mingled with the color of autumn leaves, how he had tried to imagine the people who would live in a place with such a name, as he held his breath from one end of it to the other.

When he found the town again he was disappointed. Its eighteenth- and nineteenth-century colonial houses were in need of coats of paint. Nearly all of them remained white but had gathered, especially in the eaves, carbon from an ever-increasing number of cars and diesel trucks. The houses were set too near the road now that it had been widened. The grass in their small front yards was matted and brown. Many of the maple trees that lined the only street had been cut down and others had been badly limbed on one side in order to make way for larger trucks and power lines. The streets were still stained with salt from the winter. The general store, set in a fork in the road, now had an ugly green and gold aluminum Coca-Cola sign above its door. There were a few new houses, all of them of a modern design that detracted further from the dignity and unity of the town.

He drove through the town. then turned off the highway onto a narrow dirt road and crossed a small bridge over a brook that was still receding from the spring thaw. Mud splashed and grabbed the tires of his old Nash as he fishtailed uphill. He passed two tar-paper shanties. The front yard of one was covered with old cars that had obviously broken down, one at a time, beyond repair; rusted and hunched over flat, bald tires they bore license plates dating back ten years. In the yard of the other stood a ruddy-looking boy of about five. He held a saw that was nearly as long as he was tall, ran it across a strip of plywood, pretending to saw, and glanced up at Josh's car with a distrustful expression that, too, seemed to be a parody of someone older.

He passed several farmhouses, looking for one that was vacant. All of them showed signs of life: a trickle of smoke from a chimney, a dog or cat upon the porch, a car or bicycle, a tire hanging from a tree or a child's toy broken and lying near the road. Few of them had been kept in repair. Cockeyed barns were kept from collapse by two-by-fours leaning against their rippling boards. Some of the farmhouses were only partially repainted, usually in areas most visible from the road. One had been resurfaced entirely except for the framework of its windows and doors which shown like ugly dents or gaping holes.

Meadows were overgrown. Stone fences stretched through dense scrub over land that had once been pasture. He came upon only two working farms with cattle lingering near their barns in late afternoon and fields that were not yet harrowed or planted with corn. The rest were merely homes for people who worked elsewhere or perhaps could not find work at all; each of these had gardens in which a modest assortment of vegetables could be grown.

He stopped and knocked at the second farm he encountered. A woman appeared at the window of the frame door, two small children straggling and then hiding behind her. When she saw him she stood motionless with her hand on the knob. He spoke loudly but was careful not to shout, explained that he was looking for a farm and asked her if she knew of any that were for rent. She shook her head nervously and herded her children into another room. He waited, but she did not return.

He wound along a network of dirt roads, turning instinctively down one, continuing straight when it intersected another. He found one small, abandoned farm, its windows shattered and its roof precariously near collapse. He stopped and peered through one of its windows, knowing before he did that the place was beyond repair. As he drew further from the town he passed three more farmhouses that appeared in disuse, but the land around them was hopelessly mired in a second growth of birch and poplar. The barns of two were merely heaps of rubble out of which a few rotting vertical beams rose.

The sun set, a wind rose and warned him of an advancing storm. He ate a dinner out of cans, cooked over an open fire beside a stream below the road, then drove on in the dark. He came to a paved road, realized it was the one that had led him to town, crossed it and drove uphill again. A fine mist began falling. The worn blades of his windshield wipers left a film which distorted the few lighted windows he passed. Then, finally, it rained in sheets and streaks that seemed to freeze in his headlights, nearly hypnotizing him and making him forget at times that he was looking for anything. When a deer's fluorescent eyes emerged from it suddenly, he slammed the brakes, then eased the car gently to a stop.

The doe tried to run but seemed unable to, as though her slim, delicate legs were rooted to the ground. Then, fascinated by the light, overwhelmed by it, she merely cocked her head and stared. Beneath her lay what appeared to be a broken sack of grain. As Josh stepped slowly out of the car and moved toward her, she remained transfixed, blinded by the light that was captured in traces of gray and white fur upon her belly and thighs. She had suffered through the winter. Her ribs showed. There was a scar on her left foreleg and another on her thigh.

He walked in an arc in order to avoid passing between

her and the headlights. The rain ran down his forehead into his eyes; it seemed to crystallize in the light and formed a partial curtain between them. She flinched at his moving shadow but still did not run. About ten yards from her, he let his eyes fall on the sack and saw that it was a dead fawn. He knelt slowly and stared at it. Its spots shown. Its head was curled toward its belly. Three of its legs lay stiff and straight but the fourth was impossibly twisted and nearly severed at the shoulder. There was a deep ugly gash in its neck.

When he glanced up, the doe was staring directly at him with glowing, questioning eyes. His breath stopped. He remained utterly still, but, suddenly, she wheeled and ran. He watched her disappear into the woods, her white tail bobbing, then knelt beside the fawn and put his palm against its belly. It was still warm. Its small eyes, turned away from the headlights, were black and unfathomable. The blood on its smooth fur was diluted by the rain. He carried it to the side of the road and laid it in the darkness behind a stone fence where the woods began. Then, in a rivulet, as he washed the blood from his hands, he thought he saw the doe's eyes gazing at him again from the woods, but in a split second they were gone. He stood in the rain for nearly a minute, staring toward the woods, but did not see them again.

He drove for about two miles. Then, exhausted and chilled, and feeling that the carrion of the fawn was far enough behind him, he pulled off the road. He climbed into the back seat, slid beneath a musty quilt and fell asleep to the beating of rain upon the roof.

The girl hesitated near Josh's car. With her hands on her hips, she studied the out-of-state license plate. She was about nine years old, but tall for her age and very slim. She wore jeans and a frayed white shirt that might once have belonged to her father or an older brother. Dark, wavy hair trimmed neatly about halfway down her long neck made her appear even taller. Her long, narrow face seemed always to have worn the expression of a woman much older. She pressed her nose against the window and rapped it gently with her knuckles.

Josh was not sure whether he had awakened out of a nightmare or whether the sensation of it had lingered from hours or nights before. Several moments passed before he realized that there was someone outside the car. Squinting in the sunlight, he rolled the window down.

"I'm sorry to wake you up, but you looked awfully hot in there."

"I was."

"Why did you have the window closed?"

"It was raining when I went to sleep."

"You've been here that long?"

"Yes."

They studied one another. Josh smiled, but she merely stared at him curiously.

"Do you always sleep in a car?"

"No."

"I bet it's really uncomfortable."

"It is."

He took a canteen from the floor and climbed out of the car. He poured water into his hand, ran it across his face and down the back of his neck. She asked if he was a boy or a girl. He told her that he was a boy. She said that he looked more like a boy than a girl, added that *she* looked more like a boy than a girl, too, but was a girl. He laughed.

He asked how she had found him. She pointed down the road. He saw a two-room shanty set below the road, tar-papered, with a small front porch. When he asked if she knew of any vacant farms nearby, she said that she did not but that he could ask her father.

"He likes people," she said, understanding his hesitation, "most people, anyway."

She asked if he had hurt himself, nodding toward the blood on his sweat shirt. He told her about the fawn he had found in the road.

"You'd better go ahead while I change," he said.

"I'll wait. I'm not shy, as long as it's just your shirt. I see my father naked all the time."

He laughed and prodded her with his eyes until, finally, she smiled.

She strode ahead of him up the road as he tucked in his clean work shirt and struggled to keep up with her. Glancing over her shoulder, she asked why his hair was so long. He told her that it kept the flies out of his ears. She nodded.

"You needn't worry," she explained. "There aren't many flies in Vermont this time of year."

Her father, too, was gaunt and austere. He had a long, ruddy face and jutting chin, the type of dark, heavy beard that makes a man's face appear stark and unnatural when it is freshly shaved. He sat at a linoleum-covered table before a cup of coffee and an empty plate. He seemed surprised but not disturbed at his daughter's entrance with a stranger.

"What's your name?" the girl asked. "I'm Rebecca Bickford."

He told her his name, and she introduced him to her father. The man extended his hand but did not rise. He studied Josh's hair.

"He's looking for a farm. You can help him while I fix him breakfast." Josh told her not to, but she ignored him.

"Whose place are you looking for?" Bickford asked.

"No place in particular. I'm looking for a place to rent."

Bickford merely nodded.

The two men sat across from one another, each avoiding the other's eyes. Josh did not know what to say, felt caught within the quiet, and unwanted. It seemed that Bickford had no intention of making conversation. Josh glanced around at the house. The inside was prim and neatly painted beige. The kitchen was part of the living room, and an aluminum bathtub sat in the opposite corner. There were hand-sewn gingham curtains. There was a day bed covered with a bright red corduroy bedspread; patches were neatly sewn over the tattered arms of a sofa and easy chair. Everything about the room conveyed warmth and care. An old refrigerator hummed erratically while the girl cracked eggs over an iron pan. He looked briefly at Bickford out of the corner of his eye—the way he stared at his plate and played with his fork—and realized that the man was painfully shy.

"Josh found a dead deer and carried it off the road. He was all covered with blood."

"A couple of miles from here," Josh added.

"Hit by a car?" Bickford asked, looking at Josh carefully.

"It must have been."

"A lot of them hit around here. They'll hang around on the roads looking for salt even after the winter. You have to watch where you're going."

Josh thought Bickford was intimating that he had hit the deer, but said nothing. The girl served him eggs, toast and coffee, then sat on the edge of the sofa and watched him eat, as if he were a younger brother entrusted to her care.

"Aren't any farms that I can think of," Bickford said after a while. "How much land do you need?"

"Enough to feed ten people."

"Is that all?" Bickford grinned. "You got a family?"

"No."

Bickford waited for Josh to explain but did not seem offended when he didn't. He had guessed Josh's plan.

"I'm not sure, either, who would rent to you. People around here are funny about strangers."

"Are you a native?"

Bickford shook his head. The two men grinned at one another briefly in mutual understanding.

"We've lived here about four years. I thought it would be better for her than the city," he added absently, as though making reference to their poverty.

The girl cleared and wiped the table, then filled their cups with coffee.

"What about Ritter's old farm?" she asked.

"The farm or the cabin?"

"The farm." She frowned at her father gently. "He wants a farm, Daddy, not a cabin."

"That's fine, but he uses that place for migrant workers in the fall." He turned to Josh. "He's got orchards, the biggest for miles."

"The migrants could stay in the cabin," said the girl.

"They could stay with us," Josh added.

Bickford thought for a moment, then shrugged and grinned.

They drove about a quarter mile in the direction of town. The girl signaled, Bickford turned right and Josh followed them on a seemingly endless ascent on an even narrower dirt road. Both cars rattled over a plank bridge, and the woods changed abruptly to orchards; row after row of trees with short, twisted trunks stretched away from them down a sloping field. Their bare branches were so tangled that they looked more like bushes or giant brambles than apple trees. Here and there a split trunk or branch lay upon the ground or dangled toward it, interrupting the symmetry of the evenly spaced trees.

The farmhouse was set at the summit of the mountain, above the road and about twenty yards away from it. It was a simple, two-story frame structure with a large front porch. It was tilted on its stone foundation. Its roof was bowed but freshly shingled, though its clapboard walls had weathered so that only a trace of white paint still showed. Its screen door dangled by a single hinge; two frame windows had been broken by vandals.

Behind the farmhouse were about ten acres of open field. A barn across the road was set amidst the apple trees. An orange jack-o'-lantern was painted on one of its sliding doors; beneath it, in awkward, hand-painted letters were the words "The Great Pumpkin."

"He's a funny man," Bickford said, describing Ritter. He nodded toward the jack-o'-lantern. "Some people think he did that. I doubt it—it was probably kids—but I wouldn't put it past him."

The three of them stood on the porch gazing over the orchard. Beyond it was the valley, and beyond the valley was a spectacular view of rolling brown hills that ran like the waves of a raging ocean for perhaps fifty miles.

"It's beautiful! Perfect!"

Bickford nodded, but glanced doubtfully at one of the rotting beams that supported the porch roof.

"Can you afford a tractor?"

"Maybe an old one."

"You'll need one. Do you know anything about farming?"

"No."

Bickford grinned. "Neither do I. I guess you'll learn. Nobody's lived here in winter since we've been around. There's probably no heat except a fireplace and a stove."

"That'll do."

"You wait till winter!" Bickford laughed.

He gave Josh directions to Ritter's. Josh thanked him. Both he and the girl shook his hand, then Bickford put his arm around his daughter and led her down the yard. He glanced up at the house before climbing into his car.

"If it doesn't work, stop down! Maybe I'll think of something."

Josh thanked him again.

Chapter Two

The road continued on a vague ascent for about a hundred yards beyond the farm, descended sharply, then nearly leveled again as it began to wind around the mountain. On the left the orchard ran without relief. On the right the woods gave way to a pasture in which Ritter's farmhouse stood. It was similar to dozens he had seen the day before, a two-story frame structure with three additions, each smaller than the one before, extending away from the road like boxes arranged in a row. Its white paint was cracked, eroded and covered with a film of dust churned up from the road each summer. Beside the house was a barn. Behind the barn was a single-story concrete warehouse in which apples were stored.

Ritter sat on the bottom step of a side porch near the driveway, hunched over a newspaper. He appeared older than the oldest apple tree, as skeletal and parched. The leathery, overlapping flesh of his face resembled intricate erosions on a bare hillside. His dry, brown lips, sucked into his gums, were barely visible. He wore faded blue overalls and a double-breasted, brown suitcoat that was faded and stretched.

He sat like a beggar; his knees were small bumps beneath his overalls, and the ankles inside his nylon socks were so thin that they might be shattered by the weight of his own body. He glanced up and squinted as the car approached, then frowned at Josh as he walked up the drive. He did not rise and showed no sign of interest or surprise, merely folded his newspaper and laid it beside him on the step.

"Do you know who won the race?" he asked, rasping as he tried to shout.

"No."

"No? No!" Hunched over the step, his small brown hands planted upon his knees, he glared up at Josh incredulously.

"No? You know which race I'm talking about?"

"No."

"Then what'd you say 'no' for?" He was profoundly annoyed. "Why didn't you ask me which race? You might know who won it if you knew which race! How do you know? I might be asking about a race you went to see yourself ten years ago?"

"Which race?"

Ritter paused and ran his tongue across his lips as though savoring a morsel of food.

"The human race."

His dry lips slowly curved into a grin. He began to chuckle, his small delicate frame bouncing upon the step as Josh laughed with him. Then he coughed, suddenly and uncontrollably, spat an amoeba-like glob of green phlegm, wiped his mouth with a limp, gray handkerchief and stared impatiently at Josh.

"What do you want?"

"You own the farm on top of the mountain?"

"I do, but it's not for sale. That what you're after?"

"Would you rent it?"

"I might, but I doubt it. What'll you pay?"

"I don't know."

"Come back when you do. It would have to be a lot before I'd let it go. I use it sometimes in the fall. What do you want it for?"

"A commune."

"A what?"

"A commune."

"Commune," Ritter muttered, then glanced up at Josh with renewed interest.

He reached into the pocket of his coat and pulled out a wrinkled pack of unfiltered cigarettes. He took one out of the pack, straightened it, and hunched over it with his hands cupped as he lit it, as though there were a wind.

"How many of you?"

"Maybe ten."

"They all look like you?" He nodded at Josh's hair.

"Not all of them."

"Most of them?"

"Yes."

Ritter thought for a moment and grinned coyly at his cigarette.

"Sit down," he said, "and tell me exactly what you plan to do."

Ritter listened, intermittently nodding and sucking at his cigarette. When Josh had finished Ritter abruptly changed the subject.

"You an Indian?"

"No."

"Imagine you are and don't know it. There are a lot of people that way." He paused and scrutinized Josh, who was seated on the ground.

"You're part Indian. I can tell by your color and your cheekbones. Can always tell that way. I'm part Indian, too," he added, "one-fourth Cherokee. What tribe are you?"

Josh shrugged helplessly. Ritter answered for him.

"Maybe Cherokee. We may be from the same tribe. They say you can tell by looking at the feet, but I don't feel like taking off my shoes."

His small, bony shoulders rose and fell as he sighed. He grimaced at his cigarette.

"Only one full-blooded Indian left around here. He runs a gas station over in Simpsonville." Ritter shook his head pitifully, then looked directly at Josh.

"I'll let you have it."

"What?"

"The farm! What do you think?"

Josh ran his fist across his chin and grinned.

"But you won't raise enough up there to live. Not if there's going to be ten of you. How'll you pay the rent?"

"We'll work around if we have to."

"Work's scarce up here. And even when there is work, you'll be the last to get it."

"We'll manage."

"Maybe you will. Maybe not."

Ritter took slow, even breaths and frowned, annoyed at the wheezing in his chest. He thought for a moment, then spat.

"You see those apple trees?"

"They're beautiful."

"Pish! Fot! They're ugly as sin this time of year. They will be pretty, though, when the leaves and blossoms come out.

"I used to work from one end of the orchard to the other between spring and fall keeping it in shape. It would take four men to do that now because men get lazier every year—me, too, for that matter—and they would charge me more than I make."

Ritter rubbed the tips of his fingers across a limp, wrinkled cheek as though nursing an aching tooth. Josh watched him closely, awed by the difficulty with which he breathed and spoke.

"Winter is hard on them. Branches split. Some of them get diseased—infertile—old—all of which is understandable. But when enough of them get that way the orchard's just a graveyard." He sighed. "Looks like a graveyard, too, a lot of dead trees in rows.

"Dead ones have to be cut down. The rest need pruning. New ones have to be planted. A lot more has to be done than I feel like mentioning." He glanced sharply at Josh. "How much of that you think I can still do?"

"A lot of it, I imagine," Josh lied.

"Fot! Poof! I'm seventy-seven years old! I've got a hard enough time keeping the flesh on my bones. What are you smiling at? You think it's funny?"

"No."

"Hah! Pruning, cutting, mowing, planting—you can help with the picking. I don't spray because I don't

16

believe in it, but there's still enough work for ten of you. You interested?"

"Yes."

"Do it and I'll give you the farm rent-free, use of all my equipment and fifty dollars a week. Fifty dollars a week among ten of you is only five dollars a week apiece, but that's all I can afford."

"That's all we need. It's perfect."

"We'll see. We'll see if it is," Ritter added caustically. "So, it's a deal?"

Josh nodded and smiled.

Ritter ground out his cigarette with the sole of his shoe then stared at the shreds of paper and tobacco. His head began bobbing involuntarily, nodding at the thoughts that were passing through his mind. He spoke again, more quietly and easily than before.

"I planted them all—hate to watch them go to hell, even though I know they're going to go there with me when I die. Hate to watch it for a lot of reasons, not the least of which is a lot of people around here don't mind watching it at all."

"Why?"

"Don't you know?"

Ritter stared at Josh angrily with small, penetrating eyes. Josh concentrated on a dead blade of grass that he spun between his fingers. He glanced up at Ritter and nodded.

"I know you know. If I didn't think so, I wouldn't deal with you. You a hippy?" he asked.

Josh leaned back upon his hands, laughed and shrugged.

"There aren't any hippies anymore."

"You're a hippy. I've read about them. Not many of

them stray up here this far, but I've seen a few passing through. You're a hippy, but you were a soldier, too, not too long ago. Maybe six months. About as long ago as the length of your hair."

"How did you know?"

"The way you walk and stand. And by your army shoes."

Ritter paused to light another cigarette. He packed it against the step and stared at it loathingly before shoving it between his lips.

"Were you in the war?" he asked.

Josh nodded.

"How was it? As bad as they say?"

"Worse."

"How?"

Josh remembered an old man at least Ritter's age he had seen tortured, nearly suffocated by South Vietnamese soldiers. He remembered a woman's scream from inside a burning hootch, the insane, childlike smile on the face of the American boy no more than eighteen as he trained his flame thrower on the doorway.

"I'd just as soon not talk about it. Do you mind?"

"No!" Ritter snapped. He was embarrassed. "It's your business as long as you're not a deserter. That's your business, too, for that matter."

"I'm not."

Ritter met Josh's eyes. His mood changed as abruptly as it had before. He spoke softly and with a trace of compassion.

"Good. I'm glad."

A barn swallow glided in a semicircle and settled on a fence rail across the drive. Ritter turned instinctively and looked for others that were sailing over the pasture.

He stood slowly and carefully, pushing himself up with his hands on his knees. His bones had settled and his back had bowed until he was little more than five feet tall and appeared deformed. He signaled Josh to follow him and shuffled toward a battered old farm truck parked in the barn.

Chapter Three

Ritter ordered Josh to drive.

"I used to plant corn here," he said before they drove out of sight of the meadow. "One year my whole apple crop was ruined by hail, so I started keeping cows so I wouldn't have all my eggs in one basket."

"What happened to them?"

"Got sick or died eventually, most of them, which didn't bother me because they were taking up too much of my time. Those that didn't, I sold. That was when most people started thinking I was crazy."

Josh asked why, knowing that Ritter expected him to. He remembered the Great Pumpkin, preferred to think the old man had done it but knew better than to ask him.

"I read an article in a science magazine about how you could make crops grow better by playing music to them in the morning. I'd found that hooking a radio up in the barn settled the cows down and helped them give more milk, so I thought why not try it with the corn." Hunched in the seat and leaning against the door, Ritter braced himself for potholes in the road.

"I bought a couple of loud-speakers and hooked them up to a record player. I bought some inspirational music and some band music, thinking that they would have the best effect. Played them every morning for a month loud enough so that the apple trees could hear—figured it wouldn't do them any harm either."

The left front tire caught a muddy rut and nearly forced them off the road.

"Watch where you're going!" Ritter barked. "You think it's funny? They did, too, kept laughing at me and thinking I was nuts, even in the fall when my corn was a foot taller and the ears were bigger than they had been years before.

"The first morning I played it people in town ran out on the street expecting to see a big band coming through. It echoed, you know. Some of the religious fundamentalists thought it was God himself leading a salvation army straight down out of heaven. They got mad when they found out it was just me, took me to court eventually for disturbing the peace. I think there was even talk about having me put away.

"In a nuthouse!" Ritter exclaimed. He snickered, then coughed.

He ordered Josh to stop. Josh pulled off the road about fifty yards from the old farm.

Josh walked beside the old man, who shuffled, hardly moving at times, along two ruts that had once been a road between rows of apple trees, running perpendicular to the one they had left. Ritter's neck was so stiff that he could not hold his head erect nor turn it more than a couple inches right or left. Instead, his shoulders swiveled as he glanced back and forth examining each tree perfunctorily. He pointed to the spindly branch of one tree where the shriveled brown remnants of three apples had clung through the winter to their stems.

"Couldn't get enough migrants last year," he rasped. "They don't like to come up this far for such a short season, fewer of them go to the trouble every year. Two acres of apples got frosted before we could get to them. I don't mind losing the money nearly so much as I mind the waste."

He shuffled on down the field, pointed to a dead tree, the bark of which had peeled and split revealing worm-eaten wood, nodded to another that he said had been split by an ice storm. They passed a fenced-in acre of trees that had been planted about fifteen years before. The fence, Ritter said, was to keep out the deer who would have eaten the tender bark and tips of branches when the trees were younger. Josh asked if there were many deer. Ritter said there were enough but not as many as there used to be, that more and more hunters came up from the cities each fall.

"The state's developing, too, though it doesn't look like it. Less room for them each year. Some people claim that in twenty years Vermont will be a suburb of New York. I'll be dead by then, I hope," he said dryly. "Ha! I know I'll be dead by then!"

Josh stared down the aisle of trees at the receding waves of rust-colored mountains. The world appeared, literally, to end where the earth and sky met. It did not seem possible that New York, a different world entirely, could ever bridge the cleft.

22

The path continued downhill and into the woods at the base of the orchard, then opened up again into a small field where five rows of apple trees stood, most of them dead. Their branches broken, limbs split and trunks decayed, they resembled a regiment of giant, poorly constructed scarecrows. In the bright morning sunlight they were both handsome and grotesque.

A cabin at the top of this clearing was set upon about a dozen log piles as well as pyramids of stone. The screen that had once enclosed its porch was now twisted and corroded full of holes, making the building appear more decrepit than it actually was. Its faded brown paint blended rustically with the natural color of the wood. Like that of the old farmhouse, its roof was newly shingled. Set upon the pilings, it reminded Josh of the countless shanties he had seen along highways in the deep South.

Ritter stopped near the edge of the meadow. He glanced over the old orchard, then stared for several moments at the cabin.

"I'd like to see some new trees planted here when everything else is done. And I'll pay you extra if you'll paint that shack. This was where I lived when I first came here; built it myself. Disease got those trees. I couldn't afford back then to find out what it was."

There was no trace of melancholy or sentimentality in his voice. Josh stared at the cabin, then at the old man's hunched back as he followed him back up the path.

"When did you come here?"

"Fifty-five years ago."

"From where?"

Ritter shot Josh a brief, cold stare.

The front door of the old farm was padlocked. Ritter, saying he had lost the key, borrowed a dime from Josh to unscrew the hinge, then absent-mindedly dropped the dime into his own pocket. The floor of the house slanted so distinctly that Josh had the sensation of walking up and downhill. Faded brown, flower-printed wallpaper was badly water-stained and peeling. There were gaping holes in the ceiling where plaster had cracked, or become saturated with water, and fallen. There were beds, odds and ends of dilapidated furniture, and kitchenware which Ritter said he kept there for the migrant workers. The rooms were damp and cold, stagnant and closed, void of any atmosphere that human beings might once have left.

Josh raised and lowered the handle of the pump in the kitchen.

"It'll have to be primed. You can get some water from the pond."

"Pond?"

Ritter shuffled to the kitchen window and nodded. The pond lay about fifty yards behind and to the right of the house. A small oblong body of water, it was obviously man-made. Its sparkling surface seemed like a mirage in the bleak, brown field.

"Any hair on your ass?" Ritter asked.

Josh laughed.

"Do you or don't you?"

"Not much."

"Take a cold bath each morning. Helps it grow." Ritter pecked a shriveled finger against the window pane, grinned maliciously and pointed toward the outhouse. "You'll need it this winter. And you'd better start learning to shoot your pistol fast." He shook his head and chuckled, left a film of steam on the window as he coughed.

Ritter sat on the running board of the truck and rested before climbing into it for the return trip. The bargain he had made with Josh, and simply Josh's presence, seemed to please him.

A beat-up Chevrolet rattled toward them on the road It slowed as it neared them; Ritter nodded to the two boys inside the car but, gawking at Josh, they did not notice. Josh eyed them coldly. Glancing over their shoulders as they passed, they nearly ran into a ditch beside the road.

"You know them?" Ritter asked.

"More or less."

"More or less what? Do you or don't you?" Ritter asked, annoyed.

"No."

"Then why'd you say you did?"

Somewhere down the road, the car had turned around. It approached them even more slowly. This time the boys stared intently, even angrily, as if they did know him. Ritter frowned; he stuck his thumbs in his ears and waggled his fingers at them. When they had passed again, he looked at Josh questioningly.

"I'd say they know you," he said.

Josh shook his head. He looked at the old man. Feeling that he could trust him and that he would understand, he began to tell him now how he and Pat had hitchhiked from California after Pat had been discharged. He told Ritter about the truck drivers and carloads of teenage boys that had swerved as if to hit them as they stood beside the highway, that had slowed beside and threatened them, hurled bottles and cans at them from their windows as they sped by. He told them about the gang of youths that had spotted them in a small town in Arizona, how the youths had followed and caught up with them outside it, how they had had to run and spend the night hiding in the woods.

Other things, he did not tell Ritter. They were arrested for vagrancy in Texas and handcuffed to a cell door by two policeman who intended to cut off their hair but were stopped by a superior officer who had seen some of the bad publicity such actions occasionally created. He did not tell him, nor could he remember, the number of times on the highway at night when he wondered whether he would be killed. In Oklahoma, Pat had bought a pistol, loaded it and carried it in his pocket, talking incessantly about revolution as they waited for rides.

Before they left the state, Josh had bought the Nash. The long drives in it relaxed both of them, especially at night. They would seal the windows and pass the hose of a water pipe back and forth until the smoke in the compartment was as thick as the smoke in their lungs. By the time the lights of St. Louis rose up at them, Pat had bought a shoulder holster and was pretending he was Dillinger on his way to rob the Federal Reserve.

"Maybe you ought to cut your hair," said Ritter, who was obviously not sure he believed that all those things had happened.

"Maybe I should."

"Then again, maybe you shouldn't. Maybe you ought to let it grow down to your waist." Ritter grinned at Josh slyly. Josh nodded and smiled.

When they arrived back at Ritter's farm, two palamino

ponies were hovering near the barn. They swished their tails and eyed the car dispassionately as it approached, then trotted toward the rail as it pulled in the drive. Josh asked Ritter if they were his.

"They are," Ritter spoke belligerently, as though he thought Josh were accusing him of something. Josh wondered what use the old man had for them.

"Are they draw ponies?"

"Hah!" Ritter snorted. "They draw breath! That's about it! Even act like they're putting themselves out to do that."

He frowned at them out the window of the truck. Josh asked why he had not seen them before.

"They've been over the hill. They're a he and a she. Probably messing around."

Ritter leaned his shoulder against the truck door to open it. Josh followed him over to the fence, then rubbed the palms of his hands against the ponies' pink noses as they tried to nip his fingers with their brown-stained teeth. They were fat and horribly out of shape from the long winter. Their ankles were muddy, and their backs were covered with dead grass from rolling in the pasture. They were shedding their matted winter coats, but their long blonde manes had been recently brushed and hung beautifully down their necks.

"I always wanted a couple of ponies," Ritter explained, "but never managed to get around to it. I went to a horse auction last fall—I go sometimes just to heckle the auctioneer and keep him honest—and nobody bid on these two because nobody wanted to pay to feed them over the winter. They were going to ship them on and sell them for horsemeat, so I gave them what I knew they could get."

Ritter became annoyed and embarrassed when Josh smiled at him. He reached nervously into a coat pocket and took out four sugar cubes, fed one of them to each of the ponies and hesitated before handing the other two to Josh.

"Could I ride them?"

"Doubt they'd let you. They've never been ridden and they're kind of shy." He smirked. "Some people claim to have seen me riding them, which is a lie, but I suppose it gives them a laugh."

"What are their names?"

"Call them what you want. Year with an option good enough?"

"What?"

"The lease!"

Josh nodded.

The top of the rail was the same height as Ritter's small shoulders. He put his hands on the rail and looked at the ponies, who watched him expectantly. Then he glanced down over it at his morning shadow and at Josh's, which stretched further and overlapped his own on the dead, matted grass. He nodded to them as though they were alive and had spoken, then turned and shuffled toward the house.

The ponies trotted away as Josh slid between the fence rails. They stopped when he did, but trotted away again as soon as he started for them, twisting their short, fat necks to glance back at him and contemptuously swishing their tails. Josh held out the sugar. They were interested but unwilling to approach him now that he was no longer behind the fence. The mare lowered her jaw and regarded him dolefully. The stallion cocked his head distrustfully; his nostrils flared.

Josh lay on the soft, wet ground and buried his head in his arms. The ponies eyed him skeptically, waited impatiently for him to move, then became fascinated by his stillness. Finally they gave in to their curiosity and moved toward him.

They looked down at him over their noses as if at the corpse of some strange, dead animal. The stallion nudged Josh's ribs while the mare breathed into his ear and nibbled at his hair. Josh raised his head slowly. The animals flinched and started to trot away again, then stopped as if realizing that it was too late, that they had lost the game. Josh rolled onto his back, grinned at them and extended a cube of sugar in each of his hands. They took them and greedily licked the sugar that had melted in his palms. He sat up and petted them.

Chapter Four

Ritter volunteered to pay for any materials needed to restore the farm as long as Josh provided the labor. Josh left him in the afternoon, after the old man had fed him lunch.

He spent nearly an hour inside the old farmhouse compiling a list of repairs that would need to be done. He carried water from the pond, primed the pump and ran it until clear, cold water poured freely into the soapstone sink, then washed his face and took a drink. In the late afternoon he walked through the field behind the house wondering whether they would have to clear more woods in order to raise enough food.

He walked the perimeter of the field beside uneven, tumbled-down walls of stone. He had an urge to climb the wall and walk into the woods, through the maze of bare trees and over layers of decayed leaves and rotting logs. He wanted to learn what it was about the woods that frightened him even in daylight. But he was unable to draw himself away from the farm so soon. He knelt and clawed through the grass until he held a handful of moist soil. He studied it, then smiled at himself for pretending that he knew anything about soil or farming.

He swam in the pond, then sat in the front yard with his legs crossed and watched the sunset. His mind drifted, then seemed to sink into his chest as a brilliant swell of colors became a crest of red that sharply defined the horizon before disappearing altogether. The headlights of a farm truck rumbling up the mountain jarred him out of his meditation. The barren apple trees seemed to move in the light. Their branches, like tentacles, reached out for it, casting a web of shadows upon one another, then cringed as the light passed them.

He cooked his dinner over a fire in the front yard. When he had finished eating he lay beside the fire and stared at it. It occurred to him that he had built it instead of using the wood stove because he felt alien and trapped within the scarred, empty walls of the house. As the fire died, he realized that he had been hovering near it because he was afraid of the dark. It seemed to him that this fear was a part, too, of a feeling of freedom unlike any he had ever known, and he realized that these two fears were inexplicably tied together. He listened to the droning of frogs near the pond.

He carried a mattress from one of the bedrooms into the living room and laid it on the floor, choosing to sleep in this room because it was largest, had more windows and a door. He wrote letters by candlelight, then lay, with his arms folded behind his head, listening to the walls settle. He watched the moon through a window until it was hidden behind clouds, then fell asleep.

The boy drove into the orchard and parked. He was no more than sixteen, and the girl he was with was at least two years younger. He put his arm around her and led her up to the farmhouse. He slid his hand down her small rump, then between her legs and goosed her. She giggled and he grinned, but neither of them spoke, nor did they notice Josh's car in the darkness on the other side of the barn.

Josh was awakened by the squeaking and rattling of the kitchen window as it opened. He lay nearly paralyzed with fear, as someone began clambering into the house.

"Who's there?" He moved quietly toward the kitchen, thinking it might be Ritter playing a prank.

The boy fell out of the window. The girl started to run. He signaled her to wait, licking his lips nervously.

"Who is it?" he called back.

Josh paused at the doorway to the kitchen and listened.

"It's me," he said finally.

Having no idea who it was, but assuming that he was supposed to, the boy did not ask again.

"Let's go!" the girl pleaded.

"Shh! Wait a minute." He moved closer to the window. "How long you going to be?"

"Quite a while," Josh answered.

"You mind if we come in?"

"Yes."

"Aw, come on. You don't need the whole house.

Candy's got to be home by midnight. Come on. What the hell, we won't even listen," he grinned at the girl, who was pouting.

Josh opened the door and, naked, stood grinning at both of them.

"Sorry. No vacancy."

The girl ran screaming. After a brief, incredulous stare, her boyfriend stumbled after her.

Josh learned out the front window laughing as the car spun out of the orchard.

Chapter Five

Pat and Josh had shared a corner of a thirty-bed ward at the base hospital in Honolulu. During the first morning of their confinement together, annoyed at their lack of privacy, they had regarded one another with a mixture of resentment and distrust. But, soon, discovering how much they had in common, they wondered whether the hospital had a policy of grouping undesirables together. Above all, they both detested the war and the effect that military life had had on them, the mindless regimentation and, especially, the drying up of any human feeling whatsoever as one saw so many people murdered. Both swore they would never take part in the war again, and each was appalled by the memory of the person he had been before, the one who had allowed himself even to be drafted. However, while Josh dwelt with quiet contemplation that often verged on suicidal depression, Pat regarded it with a bitterness that he frequently directed at the other patients and anyone wearing a uniform, including the nurses.

Pat was a painter. During his first two weeks in the hospital he had lain in bed drawing grotesque sketches of the doctors, nurses and Josh, and had hung them on the sterile walls in order to taunt and humor Josh out of his moods. With a dozen shrapnel wounds Pat had still been up and about the grounds much earlier then Josh, who had been shot both in the abdomen and in the calf of his left leg. He had waited on Josh, buying him cigarettes and magazines and signing out books for him at the library. He had also awakened him from his frequent nightmares. Within an hour of his first visit to town he had bought an ounce of hashish from a lanky private in a bar who, as they drank, claimed that he was only dealing temporarily in order to fly his girl friend over from Detroit for a vacation before he returned to the States.

At night Pat would push Josh in a wheel chair out onto a verandah and they would light the water pipe, waving the sweet pungent smoke away from them with fans. It was here, as they sat whispering after the rest of the ward was asleep and footsteps of the nurses on the linoleum hallway inside grew less frequent, that they had decided to start a commune and had imagined together how it would be.

They began also to formulate plans for aborting their service in the army. Nearing the end of his confinement Pat, stoned, began strolling the halls naked each night. The first time the nurses cornered him and nervously asked what he was doing, he cowered, shielding his genitals, and explained that he must have been sleep-walking. On the last night, however, he strolled out of the elevator on the first floor and nodded to the elderly nurse at the desk as he walked out the door. When two attendants took after him, he led them on a foot race around the base. When they finally caught and began questioning him, he explained he was a newborn baby and was running away from his mother who refused to feed him by breast.

Later, pacing nervously before a psychiatrist, he changed his story. He said he had come to the hospital to visit his wife and newborn boy and was merely leaving when the attendants started after him. When asked why he ran he explained that he was afraid he was going to be raped. When asked why his first story was different he said he had been confused. The psychiatrist hissed at him obscenely and threw him out of the office.

Pat was released from the hospital. Josh was released two weeks later. They were able to spend half of their thirty-day Rest and Recreation together. They bought civilian clothes, rented motorcycles and searched for secluded beaches, avoiding the hordes of servicemen with whom they did not want to be identified, pretending they spoke only Polynesian whenever a naïve group of tourists asked them for directions. Both of them had accumulated back pay which they horded for the future and both applied for disability.

At the end of these thirty days Josh told his commanding officer that he would no longer wear a uniform. After visiting several psychiatrists and remaining adamant through numerous threats of court-martial, the army suddenly and quietly granted him a discharge which stated, in effect, that the war had driven him crazy. He was satisfied with this, agreed wholeheartedly and was happy to have any blot on his record that would make it difficult for him to get a respectable job.

Pat, meanwhile, returned to duty. He had only five months left to serve but was determined not to complete them. Whenever alone, he drew chalk sketches on the walls of the barracks of men and women copulating in bizarre positions. One evening he stole into a office that housed most of the photographic equipment for the base. He rigged up a camera, stripped off his clothes and pulled a string that tripped the shutter. Before dawn he managed to print more than 300 eight-by-twelve glossies of himself bent over and grinning upside down between his legs with his anus glaring at the camera like the hairy, brown eye of a Cyclops. Before leaving he drew a sketch on the wall of himself fornicating with his sergeant.

The following afternoon he mailed the glossies to every officer with whom he had been in contact and distributed the rest to the members of his company. Each picture bore his signature, but it was not necessary, for the sketch he had drawn had been a commendable reproduction of himself. He was beaten senseless by his sergeant before being hauled to the brig.

Seated before the psychiatrist, he was intermittently pensive and distraught. He begged the man not to have him discharged, explaining that he wanted to return to the war zone and kill the gook who had shot the genitals off his best friend. The psychiatrist, believing he had found a route to the heart of Pat's problem, handling a photograph in front of him, asked Pat why he was so absorbed by the private parts of the body. Pat, trying to be helpful, explained that, as a precocious child he had read *The Sun Also Rises*. After ensnaring Pat in a critical discussion of Hemingway, the psychiatrist again threw him out of the office.

Pat was court-martialed, given a three-month sentence and a dishonorable discharge. The brig was already over-crowded with recruits who had committed every imaginable petty crime in order to delay their shipment to the war zone. In view of both this and Pat's combat record, his sentence was suspended.

He met Josh in San Francisco. They hitchhiked East and found a two-room apartment in the East Village which they opened up to anyone who needed a place to sleep. Josh took a part-time job as a janitor of their tenement and the one adjoining. Pat worked evenings as a dishwasher. They settled in for the winter, made friends and continued making plans.

When an old hearse glided into Heartwell with a sunflower wired to its antenna, a few elderly residents of the town, who never failed to read the obituaries, spotted it through their windows and wondered why they had not heard that another friend had died. The proprieter of the general store, a gaunt, gray man who seemed never to have been outdoors, regarded it soberly as it pulled up to the curb. When Pat, with a well-hewn Fu Manchu moustache, and eight other youths piled out of the hearse and through his door he stared at them with a mixture of horror and contempt. A man and woman who were shopping paused and watched. The youths fanned out down the aisles and began gathering bread, milk, cheese and fruits for lunch. They laughed. One of them tossed a pineapple to another. The proprietor, apparently afraid that he was being looted, hurried toward them frantically.

"Put that back!" he shouted. "This isn't a gymnasium!"

"We want to buy it."

"Then buy it! Buy it and get out!"

They set the food on the counter. Each of them contributed a few coins toward the total cost. Pat took a slip of paper from his pocket and read it.

"We're looking for the Old Stage Road," he said.

The man started to give directions then hesitated and looked at Pat distrustfully.

"Who you looking for?"

"You wouldn't know him."

"I would if he lives anywhere near here."

Disliking the man and aware that he was intensely curious, Pat began to tease him.

"I'll bet you wouldn't."

"I don't bet," the man said dryly.

"Never mind. Thanks anyway."

They started to leave. The proprieter followed him.

"I know everyone who lives up there. Who you looking for?"

"It's near a big orchard."

"Ritter's?"

Pat glanced at the slip of paper and nodded. The proprieter turned knowingly to his customers before giving Pat directions.

"Is that your hearse?" asked the man who had been shopping.

"It's mine," answered Jerry, a tall, lean boy with shoulder-length blond hair.

"You think that's what a hearse is for?" he said angrily. "I'll bet there's a law against using it like that."

"I'll bet there isn't," Pat answered.

"There oughta be!"

Pat frowned at him then followed the others out of the store. The tall boy stood on the roof of the hearse amidst the baggage, posing like a sailor at the helm. As the hearse roared away from the curb, he fell backward, denting the roof, then clung to a metal rack as his hair fluttered in the wind.

The proprietor, standing in the doorway, winced.

"Ritter," muttered the man behind him, "must be having a family reunion."

Meanwhile, the elderly residents of the town were phoning one another in a vain attempt to learn which of them had died. One finally called Roberta Sheldon, the town clerk, whose home and office was next door to the general store. She explained what had happened, and the information was conveyed along the grapevine; a few of the most feeble-minded were unable to understand; to them a hearse could only mean one thing.

When they reached the top of the mountain they were jubilant at the sight of the farmhouse, the orchard and the view. Even Pat, who prided in being a pessimist, could not help smiling and nodding. Josh, standing on the front porch, grinned and raised his hand in the sign of peace.

"Say, old codger!" Pat shouted. "Could you direct me to that commie plot of a hippy commune?"

"Keep going, you dirty freaks!" Josh called back. "We don't want your kind up here."

The tall boy atop the hearse shook his fist. Then he took a tabla from beneath a tarpaulin and began beating it rhythmically.

"Wow! Listen to that echo!"

It sounded as though the earth itself was throbbing.

The following morning they drove to Simpsonville for paint and other supplies that the general store did not stock. On the way back, halfway up the mountain road, Pat stopped the hearse while Maureen and Josh climbed onto the roof. They lay with their chins on their crossed arms laughing and taking deep breaths of fresh air as the hearse rattled over potholes. Buds had broken; their blood-red shells gathered in pools upon the road. Maureen picked a stem from a branch that ran across their backs, studied its small leaves then handed it to Josh. She pointed suddenly toward a large buck, with small white spikes protruding from its forehead, that was zig-zagging away from them through the apple trees.

"I've never seen one before," she said. "I thought they were like gazelles, you know, storybook things for kids." She wiped her dark curls from her face and smiled at Josh like a child. Tall and well-built, with dark weathered-looking skin, Maureen resembled a country girl but had been out of New York City very few times in her life. They glanced over their shoulders as though expecting the deer to reappear. Josh decided not to tell her about the fawn.

They found two ladders in the barn and borrowed two more from Ritter. Everyone painted. They painted designs on one another's foreheads and cheeks. Those painting on ladders dripped paint on those who were beneath. They ran dripping red fingers through one another's hair. On the boys' bellies the girls painted faces with red cheeks that puffed and smiles that extended each time the boys inhaled. Pat painted a nude with flaming hair and distended breasts on Josh's back. No one would tell him what it was until, finally, he went into the house and stared over his shoulder at a mirror.

They also painted the house. Pat, with the artist's touch and an unwillingness to slap paint on walls, worked with Josh trimming the window frames and doors white as soon as the red paint set. Peter, a shy, sandy-haired boy, with a pale, handsome, almost feminine face, worked quietly beside his girl friend Mary on the back wall. Peter and Josh had met in New York soon after Peter was released from Allentown where he had served two years as a C.O. There, Josh guessed, was where Peter had acquired the stoop in his shoulders and the look in his eyes that made him seem so much older.

Cyndee, a short, plump girl with naturally platinum hair cropped just below her ears, served beer and fed sandwiches to boys whose hands were sticky with paint. Jerry, the tall boy who always wore a dull smile, appeared on the porch with Maureen, who had drawn designs resembling war paint on his body and face. They performed an anti-rain dance though the pale clouds posed no threat, Maureen rattling beads, Jerry beating his tabla and shaking his hair as they chanted a rhyme they had learned as children.

> Rain rain go away
> Come again some other day
> Rain rain go away
> Go away go away.

When a truck slowed as it passed and its driver stared goggle-eyed, they laughed and bowed as if performing from a stage.

By late afternoon they had finished. Pat lay with is

head on a stone languidly sipping a beer and stirring a half-empty can of paint; when a carload of youths passed and cursed at the house he halfheartedly gave them the finger. Maureen and Mike, a well-built Jewish boy with dark, curly hair, who had been disowned by his parents for living with a Catholic girl, lay asleep on the porch with their arms around one another. They bore such a strong resemblance to one another that, even when holding hands, they looked more like brother and sister than lovers. Rodney, a draft dodger whose real name was James, sat on the porch steps sharing a joint with Jerry; small, with long wavy hair, bushy eyebrows and a goatee, he resembled, as always, a scientist absorbed in his work.

The farmhouse had been transformed. Indian music oozed out its open windows; its new red coat of paint, still wet, shown like lacquer in the sunlight. It was now a handsome place, if cockeyed, and to the native passerby it would seem both a familiar house and one that had appeared from nowhere.

Chapter Six

Early the next morning they brought the tractor up from Ritter's. Ritter drove. Pat and Josh stood behind him holding onto the rusty seat, shirtless and swaying as Ritter maneuvered around ruts, watching the ponies trot beside them on the other side of the fence to the end of the field. The painted faces on their backs and bellies had blocked out the sun the day before so that the features still showed though they were now white upon burnt red skin.

They had had to change the spark plugs, tinker with the carburetor and prime it before the engine would run. It spewed black smoke, sputtered and galloped, then seemed to adjust itself, or resign itself like a nag that had merely been reluctant to leave the barn, while Ritter ground into lower gears as they crept up the last stretch of mountain.

Ritter squinted up at the farmhouse and frowned.

"That my place?"

"Looks a little different, doesn't it?" Pat beamed.

Ritter snorted. "Ha! I say you could paint it that color?"

Josh and Pat glanced at one another behind the old man's back, then Josh explained that they had forgotten to ask.

"Forgot!" Ritter looked up at the farmhouse again, then sniffed and rubbed his nose. "I figured you'd asked and I'd probably forgot. My mind slips, you know. Paint it purple! I don't care," he muttered. "Fix it up too much, though, I might sell it."

He waved his arm, dismissing it, then clutched the wheel with his withered hands as though at ten miles an hour he was capable of losing control.

"Pay you to paint my place sometime; I'm sick of white. Paint it like a big peacock! Give people something else to talk about."

He snorted and laughed, then coughed into his lap. The commune seemed to have already worked a change in him. He asserted his eccentricity with a renewed fervency, even belligerence, acting at times like a child who had finally broken away from home. He smiled more and was obviously enjoying himself on the tractor.

Nearly everyone stood on the front porch or in the yard waiting as the tractor pulled off the road and traversed the slope leading up to the field. They followed it until Ritter eased it to a stop and let the engine die. Josh introduced Ritter to those he had not met, but Ritter had no patience for introductions. He nodded his head several times for every name that was spoken, stared harshly at each smiling face and ignored the hands that were held out to him. He did not react to even the most bizarre physical characteristics of the group except to give Jerry's pale, sticklike body and shoulder-length hair one brief, awful stare.

Josh had asked him to supervise because no one knew how to operate farm equipment. Ritter stood by the plow and explained how it was manipulated from the tractor, using the flat of his hand to illustrate how the blade should lacerate the earth. He stared at them as he spoke, as though accusing them of lacking common sense. Then, with difficulty, but unwilling to accept a hand, Ritter boarded the machine again. A shaft squeaked as it wound, and the blade of the plow sank gently to the ground. Ritter nudged the tractor forward, keenly aware that all eyes were watching him. The rusty blade cut into the soil like a razor; a strip of earth a foot wide followed the rising curve of the blade and tumbled over smoothly, as if in slow motion, so that the plow left behind it a furrow and a smooth, diagonal mound of soil. It was both a painful and fascinating process to observe.

"Worms!" Mike exclaimed. "Look at them all! God they're ugly!" This was the first time he too had been in the country, the *real* country as he called it, in his life. He held up the larger part of a worm that had been severed by the blade and displayed it to Maureen who regarded it dispassionately, then he fell to his hands and knees and stared at the back of the plow to study the way that it worked. Finally he rolled onto his back, assimilating the tumbling, spiral motion of the sod, and lay with his arms outspread staring up at the sky.

Josh remembered the field outside an Asian village that had been sprayed by American planes. Torrential monsoon rains had carried the poison deep into the ground. He had watched the villagers paw through the earth with their bare hands searching for a worm or an insect living; they had found none. It was from observing the fear and starvation in their faces, the looks of desolation in their eyes too utterly defeated to bear hatred as they stared up at him and his platoon, that he had learned how important worms were to the soil.

"Gotta watch out for stones!" Ritter rasped, but no one heard his across the field or above the engine's roar. He turned the tractor around and plowed another furrow so that the sod from this overlapped onto the first, stopped when he was before them again.

"Plow in a straight line. Raise the plow when you turn and don't set it down till you're straight again or you'll bust it every time." He made his open hand into a fist for emphasis, then eyed them dubiously as though accusing them of having broken it already. "Keep your furrows close enough so that all the ground gets turned. That means always keeping them closer together than it looks like you need to."

Josh climbed aboard, and Ritter showed him how to operate the gears before lowering himself precariously to the ground.

Cyndee carried a rocking chair off the porch and set it in the field. Ritter glared at her and refused it. After a few minutes he leaned against it, breathing in deep sighs in an effort to eliminate his high-pitched wheezing. Finally his knees gave out and he sat, looking surreal in the rocker with the plow passing back and forth before him.

"Rocks! Oww! Watch where you're going!" He shouted and winced each time the blade of the plow ground against a stone.

They plowed throughout the morning and afternoon, everyone taking a turn and learning how to operate the machinery from whoever had driven before. Ritter enjoyed watching them work, especially the girls. He sat with a large glass of iced tea in his hand, sucking and chewing on the slice of lemon, smacking his lips and hurling commands. Those who were not plowing began patching the walls inside the house. Because they had chosen to live without electricity, Peter and Mary set out in Josh's car in search of candles and old kerosene lamps. Jerry made a stack of fire pails with rope handles from old sap buckets he had found in the barn.

Cars and trucks passed the farm in numbers unusual for the rural dirt road. Somewhere beyond the farm most of them would turn around, passing it again minutes later driving even more slowly. It was Saturday. Men, in groups, or driving their wives and children, and teenage boys in beat-up coupes, stared out their windows, then glanced at one another ominously, as though witnessing a disaster beyond words. None of them stopped, though they were frequently waved at and greeted. Two teenage boys in a pickup shouted something as they sped past, but their voices overlapped incomprehensibly. Ritter appeared to recognize each of them but observed them all with equal annoyance and acknowledged each driver only by returning his stare.

In the middle of the afternoon, Josh noticed Ritter fumbling nervously with an empty pack of cigarettes and offered to drive him to town, explaining that he had planned to go anyway in order to purchase a salt lick. Ritter stared distrustfully at the hearse before climbing into it, then sat self-consciously on the foam rubber seat and tucked his hands in his lap as if to protect them from fabric and metal that was tainted with death.

"A salt lick!" he exclaimed suddenly when they were about halfway to town. "You planning to raise cattle?"

"I'm going to put it out for the deer."

"Deer?"

"I thought if I put it out near the house they might begin to come around."

Ritter drew his upper lip back above his yellow false teeth in a way that reminded Josh of the ponies when they neighed.

"What for? You nuts?"

Josh shrugged.

"Enough of them around here without putting out salt licks. They'll make a mess of your crop."

"I could put it across the road."

"In the orchard?" Ritter frowned.

"Will they hurt the trees?"

"No! No! Clap-trap!" He dismissed it with an awkward wave of his arms. "Do what you want to! I don't care!"

The proprietor, who had seen them coming, eyed them coolly as they entered the store. Ritter nodded to him and shuffled immediately up to the counter. He turned to Josh.

"You two met?"

Josh nodded. Ritter looked at the man again.

"He's been in here before," the man answered dryly before Ritter could override him.

"This is Samuel Fletcher. Be sure to call him *Mr. Fletcher* or *Samuel*. Don't ever call him *Sam*, because he thinks it's undignified."

Fletcher's eyes narrowed. Ritter grinned at him maliciously, then winked at Josh.

Fletcher waited until Josh had carried the salt lick out the door, then turned on Ritter.

"Are you crazy?"

Ritter stared at him. "No need to ask that. Is there?"

"You'd better get them out of here."

"Why?"

"You know why."

"I don't."

"Nobody wants them around here, and there are people who won't put up with it."

"They don't have to put up with anything. It's none of their business."

"Are you *trying* to cause trouble?" Fletcher exploded.

"No."

"You've *got* to be!"

"I'm not and there's no reason for anybody else to. They're a bunch of kids. They're not going to hurt anybody."

Fletcher paused to regain his temper, then tried to reason with him.

"Is the lease signed?"

"Yes."

"You can break it. Nobody would back them up."

"I wouldn't even if I wanted to, which I don't," Ritter answered calmly.

"*Why*? I don't see why you did it!"

"I lost two acres of applies to frost last year. That sort of thing never happens, but it did. It didn't have to happen."

"You didn't ask for help."

"You know why I didn't and why I never would. And

you know I shouldn't have to."

"That's got nothing to do with it!"

"It does, because it's not going to heppen again."

"Is that why you let them have it?" Fletcher asked.

"No."

"It's got to be."

"Maybe it is," Ritter added, "but not in the way you think."

"You'll be to blame if anything happens," Fletcher warned him.

"Nothing's going to happen."

"It will."

"It won't!" Ritter snarled. "Unless you stand behind there telling everybody it will!"

"I'm not saying anything."

"It sounds that way!"

"I'm not! I'm just warning you," Fletcher drew back, on the defensive.

Ritter lit a cigarette and watched the smoking match arch toward the floor. He spoke quietly, sarcastically. "Good. Thanks. I appreciate it." Then he nodded and shuffled toward the door.

A carload of youths parked across from the farm. They piled out of the car, then leaned against it and began cursing at and heckling the members of the commune. They smoked cigarettes, made jokes regarding the effeminacy of the long-haired boys, and laughed with one another. They were content to stay on their side of the road and seemed to regard the confrontation as somewhat of a lark until Pat lowered his pants, stuck his buttocks out a bedroom window above the porch and farted more or less in their faces.

Then they grew angry, began shouting at him to fight as he turned and grinned at them, and yelled at others who sat passively on the porch. Pat climbed onto the porch roof and continued to mock them. He took off his shirt and posed like a wrestler, flexing his biceps and measuring them with his thumb and forefinger.

"Come on, motherfucker! Come on down!" One of them screamed, his face red and eyes bulging. The rest of the commune gathered in the yard to watch Pat's exhibition. Some of them, amused, cheered, but others were disturbed and motioned him to stop. He ignored them.

He cupped his hand to his ear. "What'd you say?" he called back to the youths. "Didn't hear you! Something about my mother?"

"I said come on! *Motherfucker*!"

"Tut! Tut! Those are harsh words! My mother's dead! Besides, I never had the pleasure!"

Though furious, the boys were still reluctant to approach the commune. Pat began to shadow box, treating the roof as a ring, ducking and jabbing, absorbing blows from an imaginary opponent whom he finally pinned against the wall and pummeled. He pranced and raised his fist triumphantly as they cursed at him and begged him to fight, then he stared down at them, smirked and played villainously with his moustache.

"Come on down!" Maureen begged him. "That's enough!"

"Motherfucker, hey?" Pat shouted. "At least I don't seduce pubescent girls! By the way, how's Candy?" Josh had told him. The young blond boy who had tried to break into the farm blushed and fumed while the others looked at him, waiting for him to do something. Pat had only guessed that the boy was among them.

"You want to fight? Okay! But you see I'm small—one hundred forty-three pounds the last time I weighed myself. I'll tell you what I'll do," he said. "I'll take on anyone up to one hundred sixty! Step right this way."

"Come on, Pat," Peter called. "Go inside." Now all of the group stood viewing him with disfavor, sensing that his joke had gone too far.

"Come on down!" shouted the blond boy. He moved to the foot of the yard.

"Uh-uh," Pat shook his head. "Up here! A duel to the death!" He pointed toward the ground. It was at least a ten-foot drop.

"Motherfucker!"

"I'd say," Pat said sarcastically, "that you've got incest on the brain. I've heard what goes on in these rural communities."

The boy hesitated in the yard, aware that he was being made a fool of but not sure how, unwilling to climb a ladder that was resting against the roof.

"I'll fight him if you won't!" another boy said suddenly. The oldest and largest, and apparently the leader, he stroke across the road and up the yard. He had short, bristly hair, protuberant ears and the demeanor of one about to do his duty. The sleeves of his soiled T-shirt were rolled up to his shoulders. His biceps rippled impressively as he grabbed a rung of the ladder. Pat shadowboxed again, ignoring him until he was halfway to the roof. Then he scurried to the edge of the roof and shoved the ladder away. The boy screamed as it arched slowly backward, picked up speed and crushed him against the ground.

"You're too big," Pat explained as the boy lay writhing and moaning with the breath knocked out of him.

"Motherfucker," the boy moaned. His friends raced to help him.

"Next!" Pat shouted.

All of the boys of the commune, except Peter the pacifist, were furious with Pat as they braced themselves for a fight. The hearse rumbled up the road. Josh jumped out and ran toward the house. Ritter shuffled after him. Josh stared at Pat, then at the boy on the ground, trying to guess what had happened. Suddenly, a fist slammed into the side of his face. As he reeled, the three other boys pounced upon him. Pat lept from the roof, tumbled upon the ground, then ran with his head lowered and drove his shoulders into the mob. All five of them fell and tangled, fists flailing, Pat laughing and enjoying himself tremendously. Mike, Jerry and the other boys tried to pull them apart. Ritter finally reached the pile of bodies and began kicking at them indiscriminately.

"Hee! Haa!" he rasped. "Goons! Apes!"

They broke their holds on one another and rolled away from his flailing boots, then stood and formed into two groups. Ritter moved between them, wheeled and kicked one of the boys in the shin.

"Out! Out! Out!" he shouted, pursuing them as they backed angrily down the hill.

"You're trespassing! Come up here again and I'll have you thrown in jail!"

He followed them to the road, his chest heaving asthmatically. The bigger boy stopped before climbing into the car and stared past Ritter at the farmhouse.

"I'll get you, motherfucker!" he shouted at Pat.

"You'd better get out of here while you can!"

Pat grinned and waved, then gestured at him obscenely behind Ritter's back.

"Shut your mouth!" Ritter snapped. "Get out of here!"

"I'm on the road! This ain't your land!"

Ritter shuffled toward him with his fists clenched. The boy faced and stared at him angrily before sliding behind the wheel of the car. He popped the clutch; the car's spinning tires hurled gravel at Ritter's feet as it fishtailed away.

Josh noticed the way the others were frowning at Pat. "Did you start this?" he asked. Pat grinned.

"Not me. There I was just sunning myself in the window when these guys started calling for a fight. 'Am I to take this?' says I. 'No,' says I, 'somebody's got to stand up to them brutes.' "

Josh started to speak but merely looked at him. Ritter trudged up the hill, grinning victoriously now that they were gone.

"You did all right," he said to all of them, but mainly to Pat, whom he admired for his leap from the roof. "Fight like that, they'll learn to keep their distance."

After Josh had driven Ritter home, he cornered Pat alone on the porch.

"You started it, didn't you?"

Pat grinned and shrugged.

"Why?" Josh asked.

"Because I'm sick of their crap. What am I supposed to do?"

"Nothing! How long do you think we'll last up here if we start fighting them?"

"Longer than if we don't."

"Do you *believe* that?" Josh waited for Pat to answer. "They could have us out of here in a *week* if enough of them wanted to. All they need is one good excuse."

"What about Manchester and Williams?" Pat said, mentioning two communes they knew of that had been destroyed. "Did they fight?"

"It doesn't matter. That's got nothing to do with it. Those kids are going to be after us from now on, and so will the town once they hear about it."

"They were before," he answered casually. "What's the difference?"

"What did you do with that pistol?"

"I threw it away."

"You sure?"

"Listen," Pat said without answering him, "if you want to play Galahad, go ahead. But don't ask everybody else to. Remember what we said when we talked about the place: no rules?"

"I'm not talking about rules! Common sense! Just use your head."

"What's common sense? What's using my head—to let them come in here and bust it up? What about that old gook pacifist in your nightmares? How far did it get him?"

Pat, realizing he had struck a vital nerve, grinned, then felt guilty for doing so.

"Look, forget it. Okay? If they come around again I'll do the Christ thing. I'll kiss their asses. Okay? Just let it go."

Josh eyed him closely, then nodded. Pat smiled at him finally and made the sign of peace.

Chapter Seven

Ritter instructed them not to plant for at least two weeks. They ran the harrow over the field twice each day until it lay as smooth as a brown wool blanket fading in sunlight. They began restoring Ritter's orchards, chopping down dead trees, sawing off the dead limbs of others and sealing the wounds with tar. They sawed the trunks and larger limbs into even lengths, split and carried them up to the house for firewood. Maureen and Mary pruned the dead limbs they could reach, and each time a tree was felled, they planted one of several dozen seedlings that Ritter had had delivered from a large, downstate nursery.

Christine arrived on the afternoon they finally planted, small and slim and cockeyed with the weight of her suitcase. She wore chino pants, and her long red hair created a striking contrast as it streamed down her white cotton jersey. Her small face was as distinctly oval as the subject of a Modigliani painting. It was freshly burned; she blended with the blossoms on the apple trees as she trudged up the road, yet appeared to have arrived atop the mountain after making a complex series of wrong turns.

As she stopped beside the house and watched them planting by hand on their hands and knees, she thought for a moment that they were searching for something that someone had lost. She left her suitcase in the yard and walked toward Maureen, stepping carefully along an aisle between molelike mounds of soil. Maureen glanced up from her work and left streaks of mud where she wiped the sweat from her cheeks.

Christine said hello. Maureen nodded and looked at her questioningly. Others nearby glanced up from their work.

"Are you looking for someone?"

"Is this the commune?"

"Yes."

"I'd like to join or at least stay for a while." She smiled, embarrassed. "I know that's blunt but I don't know how else to put it."

Maureen smiled back at her then rose and wiped her hands on the seat of her pants. When she called Josh everyone rose and walked toward them. Josh, bare-backed and suntanned in a pair of soiled jeans, nodded to her, then looked at Maureen.

"She wants to join."

"If I can," Christine added. "Or I'd pay room and board if I could stay for a while."

"You didn't have to ask me," Josh said to Maureen.

Maureen shrugged. The others waited for him to speak.

"Where are you from?"

"Marshfield College."

"Where's that?"

"About thirty miles from here. It's a girl's college. I quit."

"I don't blame you," Maureen laughed.

"How did you hear about us?" asked Pat.

"At the college."

"How did they know?"

"Word spreads fast up here. Not much happens."

"Is the talk good or bad?" said Josh.

"It depends who you talk to. From what I've heard, people around here think they've been invaded."

"They're right!" Pat grinned malevolently. "They have."

"Will there be anyone looking for you?" Josh asked.

"No." She shook her head, then added, "I'll work. I'd like to."

"Do you have any old clothes?"

"These are all right."

"Good. I'll show you what to do."

He led her to a barrel full of dried kernels of corn and handed her a small burlap bag.

"Fill the bag." He did it for her. "Take out a handful at a time and drop groups of four about a foot apart. Don't pour them. Too many come out that way and they're wasted."

After showing her where to plant, he told her that she was welcome to stay as long as she wanted. He explained, too, that he was not the leader, that there were none, but saw in her eyes and was disturbed that she did not believe him.

She began planting in the row beside his, her hair

dangling near the ground and swaying back and forth as she crawled forward. Rodney, Mike and Cyndee, who were the least shy, came over at different times to greet her. Josh listened as they spoke but was careful only to glance at her when she wasn't looking. Once, when she was ahead of him, he watched her rub the small of her back and tie her hair with a piece of string she pulled from the lip of the burlap sack. When she turned, saw him watching and smiled at him self-consciously, he turned abruptly back to his work. They planted till sunset, paused briefly, then continued working in moonlight, determined to finish that night.

When they finished and Christine found herself beside Josh at the end of the field in the dark, she asked him jokingly whether they always worked so late. He told her that they didn't, then dismissed her in a way that she recognized as unnatural to him. She turned away, contemplating the empty burlap bag and wondering for the first time whether she was really wanted on the farm.

They walked in a group toward the pond largely because everyone was interested in finding out more about Christine. Pat hovered the nearest to her and asked the most questions, laughing childishly, as he always did when meeting a girl, and walking more erect in order to make himself taller.

She answered their questions quietly and with less confidence than she had displayed upon her arrival. Twice she glanced across the group at Josh, who took no part in the conversation. She was surprised, but tried not to show it, when they began stripping their muddy clothes. She undressed carefully and quietly with her eyes on the water, wondering if she was, in effect, being subjected to a kind of initiation.

Josh swam quickly to the other side of the pond then stood and looked for her. He waited and watched the others slip back into their clothes complaining that no one had brought towels, listened to them moaning and chattering as they ran toward the house in the brisk night air. He listened for her voice.

He swam toward shore, stopped then turned and saw her head bobbing on the surface as she kneeled in shallow water. Suddenly, Maureen and Mike hurried toward the shore, gathered their clothes and ran, laughing, across the field, leaving Josh and Christine alone at opposite ends of the pond. He realized that she had been waiting for the others to leave so that she could dress alone.

He stepped out of the pond and slid into his jeans then turned and looked for her. She stared at him questioningly. He sat on the ground with his legs crossed and lit a cigarette, waiting for her. Finally, she rose out of the pond and stood at its edge, facing him.

"Why did you do that?" she asked.

"What?"

"Wait. You knew why I was waiting, didn't you?"

He nodded.

"Then, why?"

He shrugged and smiled, staring at her body. "I'm a dirty old man."

"You don't want me here, do you?"

"Yes."

"Isn't that what you were going to tell me?"

"No."

"That's what I thought. Really. Why did you act that way?"

"Because I wanted you. Because I want you. Do you

know?"

She nodded and smiled, though she was afraid of him. She did not move or try to cover herself.

"I watched you when you got out of the water," she said quietly. "I tried not to, but I couldn't help it. Were you getting even with me by waiting?"

"No." He stood. "Do you want me to go ahead while you dress?"

She looked at him for a long time with a seriousness that seemed more and more feigned.

"I don't want to dress."

They smiled at one another, then laughed.

When they walked up the yard and into the house, everyone except Pat was careful not to stare at them. Pat lay on the porch swing with his head propped up by a pillow, sipping a pint bottle of bourbon. He eyed them with a sarcastic frown that Christine interpreted as an accusation. She was embarrassed that he knew what had happened.

Before Christine and Josh had finished cooking their own dinner, Jerry, who had majored in anthropology before flunking out of college, passed through the house telling everyone to prepare for a celebration for the Rejuvenation of Our Axis Mundi and the Rites of the Newly Sewn Seed. They laughed, then Josh looked at Christine closely.

"Don't worry," she whispered, "I won't get pregnant."

Pat appeared suddenly in the doorway. "Why not?" he asked. "We need some new blood around here."

He walked out the back door, letting the screen door slam. Christine stared after him as though she had been slapped. It was the first time Josh had ever been angry with him.

They built a fire in a shallow depression in the field near the woods. Working in half-moonlight, their sweating faces shone above armloads of branches and logs.

"You know," Pat remarked to no one in particular, "I just realized that I'm afraid of the woods at night. Ghosts and goblins and stuff like that."

They lit the fire with used paint thinner. The fire lit the edge of the woods; its flickering made them appear fluid and threateningly close. They sat with their legs crossed or lay around the fire, their shadows extending like spokes of a giant wheel. They were tired, and quiet beneath the roaring flames and crackling of wood. Their eyes watered and shone as the heat swelled against their faces. Jerry asked if anyone had anything to say.

"Say something, Josh," Maureen whispered.

Josh stood and slid his hands into the hip pockets of his jeans. The uneven light created harsh shadows on his face.

"I just want to say that I think everyone who wants to come here should be able to. Is that all right?"

Everyone nodded that it was. They glanced at Christine. Some of them smiled at her.

Mike stood. "I don't think we should call it our place. Land can't belong to you. It's everybody's. Everybody should be welcome."

"Everyone agree?" Jerry asked.

Everyone nodded. Cyndee stood as Mike and Josh sat.

"I agree," she said. "I just think we maybe should have a rule about drugs. A bust could ruin everything. It's ruined a lot of other places."

"What sort of rule?" Jerry asked distrustfully.

"Nothing, except that we should have one safe place to hide it, and that we shouldn't carry anything on us. Is that okay?"

They all agreed.

"Okay," Jerry answered, smiling at her. Standing before them in the firelight Cyndee appeared more plump and shy and younger than she was.

"Anything else?" Jerry said.

"I'm going to make pots and sell them," Maureen answered without rising. "And Pat is going to do paintings and sketches."

"Pastoral stuff and all that shit," Pat explained. "I've decided to sell out my talents."

"We'll drive around and try to get the tourist shops to sell them," Maureen added. "Does anyone else know how to make anything we can sell?"

Peter, with his arm around Mary, raised his hand meekly.

"I blow glass."

"You do *what*?" Pat asked.

"Blow glass. I learned in prison. I've got a whole kit. I've taught Mary to blow it too."

Mary, the youngest, prettiest and most taciturn of the girls, seemed small and childlike even seated between Peter and Pat. She smiled benignly and nodded in assent.

"Beautiful!" someone shouted.

"That's fantastic."

Everyone laughed.

"What's next?" Josh asked.

Jerry stood, tall and slouched, and began explaining the purpose of the ceremony. He asked them to take off their clothes and lie on their stomachs, facing the fire.

"Are you kidding?" exclaimed Rodney, who rarely said anything.

"It's getting cold," added Cyndee, who was always practical.

"I'm going to bed," said Maureen. She stood and waited for Mike to follow her. There was laughter mixed with moans of disapproval.

Jerry trotted around the fire waving his hands frantically as Josh lay laughing beside Christine.

"Okay! Forget the naked part. How about just stripping to the waist. It would help set the mood."

There were hisses and boos. Josh remarked that it ought to be enough for Jerry alone to strip. The others agreed. Someone began chanting "strip strip strip" and the others joined. Blushing, Jerry raised his hands but could not silence them. Finally, he undressed beside the fire. They cheered. The pits of his lanky arms shown like black, unfathomable jowls as he raised his hands for silence. He asked them each to find a stone and hold it in their hands, waited while they patted and groped through the grass, then lay on their bellies facing the fire. When all of them were settled he began his incantation.

He spoke of the farmhouse that had stood empty and the field that had lain barren for years, of those who had nurtured and cultivated it, then left it for the siren of advancing civilization. He spoke of a harvest of smokestacks and steel beams, missiles and monuments to war. Some snickered at his metaphors, others stifled their yawns, but he ignored them, flailing his lanky arms for emphasis like a minister engrossed by his voice.

They listened as he led them into the pine woods where, years ago, the spirit of vegetation had fled to spend the winter and had never been called again. They did not laugh as he described a kernel of corn as a congealed ray of sunlight. They turned, when he implored them to, toward the woods from which the spirit of vegetation would come. He told them that they were supposed to make a sacrifice or symbolic offering of food to the corn spirit. Rodney suggested throwing Jerry into the fire. Cyndee held out a large package of marshmallows that she had been hiding behind her back.

"We could give them some of these," she said. "I thought we'd toast them."

Jerry shook his head in despair as they laughed. Finally he took a handful of marshmallows from the bag and pierced them with the end of a stick. When lit, the marshmallows became a flare. Jerry waved it once in a circle then hurled it toward the woods. The wind extinguished it in mid-air, and it left a trail of smoke illuminated by the campfire.

"Okay," he said. "Now take the stone and hold it in the palm of your hand." He spoke softly now, smiling calmly at the fire. "Look at it and meditate on it until it means something to you."

They stared at the stones. Some of them turned them over and examined them in the light. Pat tossed his from hand to hand. Maureen closed her eyes and held hers tightly. Peter, hunched over his, stared at it sadly as though it were a bird with a broken wing. Rodney, sucking a joint, saw his glitter and imagined that he was sitting on a mountain of gold.

"Toss them into the fire when you know what they are."

The stones, thrown into the fire, unsettled a precarious pyramid of disintegrating logs. The fire rose.

Jerry raised his arms again.

"With the casting of these stones—"

"Shhhh!" Christine interrupted him. "Listen!" She nodded toward the woods past where the flare had fallen.

"There's somebody there!"

They listened to rustling leaves and broken twigs as two sets of footsteps raced away from them through the woods. No one moved except Jerry, who hurriedly dressed.

Chapter Eight

At sunrise, she leaned out the bedroom window and watched him walking through the field with his shoulders hunched against the dampness and his hands in his pockets. She watched him stare at the ground and wondered if he expected the seeds to have burst and broken through the soil overnight. She wanted to call and ask him this as a joke, but didn't want to wake the others and sensed that he was enjoying the early morning silence. His appreciation for silence was one of the two things that she understood about him. The other thing she knew, or thought she knew, was that he always understood what was going on in her mind. Not so much who she was or why she had come or any of those things; she wasn't even sure that he understood what she was thinking; it was simply that he had responded instantly to the way that she felt.

He had understood why she had paused outside his

bedroom door with her suitcase, had known that she hesitated partly for fear of intruding further into his world. In the candlelit silence of the bedroom, as they lay beside one another, he had known that she was afraid of him and had probably known why this was so even more than she had herself. He had known enough not to touch her until she had relaxed.

She had listened to the creaking of bedsprings in the next room, and he had known that this disturbed her just as she had known instinctively that it was Pat and that he was listening. He had also understood why she had asked him to let the candle burn when he had reached to put it out. He would have become a stranger in the darkness, for his eyes and his smile were the only things about him that had already become familiar.

She waited until he turned toward the house then waved to him. He walked toward the house then stood beneath the window and looked up at her. He raised a ladder that lay against the foundation, set it gently against the wall and climbed up to her. He studied her with his arms crossed on the windowsill. When she started to dress he asked her not to. She knelt and kissed him.

They left the house before anyone else had risen, walking through the woods in the direction of Ritter's farm. They came to a path that had once been a road, bounded on either side and separated from the woods by crumbling stone walls. They followed it downhill, where they found the foundations of what had been two farms. In a small clearing they found a graveyard with about a dozen headstones. A fence that had once surrounded it was rotted and fallen; the stones were visible only because the golden rod and wild grass were not fully grown.

The stones were slate, chipped and eroded so that the names and dates barely shown. Contortions of the earth's crust over generations of winters had rearranged them haphazardly so that some were tilted sideways, others slanted toward the ground. It was a family plot; there was only one name. Macabre, round faces of what were meant to be angels were chiseled upon several of the stones. Josh knelt and ran his fingers across them, reading her the names and dates.

"There is nothing here."

"Yes there is. There," she knelt beside him and pointed.

"No. That's what it says. 'Faith Chapman 1796 to 1822. There is nothing here.' Kind of depressing. Can you imagine the girl who wrote that?"

Christine sat with her legs crossed in front of the headstone and thought about it.

"She'd be pale and dark-eyed, and glum like that angel." She pressed her lips together, sucked in her cheeks and frowned, assuming an imagined expression of the dead girl.

"She'd be a virgin with no regrets," she added. "And her father was the only man she loved."

"I don't know. Maybe she was an early American Buddhist."

"Disowned for her beliefs?"

"Yes. And she died of a broken heart."

"But was given a Christian burial that saved her in the end."

They smiled. Christine paused and wound a blade of grass around her finger.

"I guess it was always like that."

He shrugged. "I guess. More or less."

There were small ferns in the clearing. A month before there had been pouches, like clenched fists, at the end of their stems as they drove through the earth. Now the many branches of each were like the fingers of a delicate, inhuman hand. Christine took off her sweater, spread it upon the ground and lay upon it. He unbuttoned his shirt and lay with his arm around her until she fell asleep.

He was nearly asleep himself when he heard something moving in the woods. He woke her and pointed to a fawn that had stepped into the clearing. Rusty brown and spotted, with long, pointed ears and delicate legs, it stopped and stared about the clearing as if lost. It saw them but seemed not yet to have developed a fear of men. Instead of running, it circumvented them slowly, staring as if trying to recognize them. Then it broke into a trot and disappeared into the woods.

"It's lost. It thought we were its parents," Christine whispered. "I really think it did!"

"I never get used to them," Josh said quietly.

"They're beautiful."

"I mean the idea of them. That there aren't any fences and no one ever sees them except by chance. It shouldn't seem strange, but it does. Do you know?"

She nodded and looked at him. With his legs crossed, staring in the direction the deer had gone, he resembled a child. She wondered how she could have been afraid of him and why, though in a milder way, she still was.

"You had a dream last night," she said gently. "A nightmare."

He glanced at her sharply, then averted his eyes, staring down at the ground.

"Did I scare you?"

"You screamed. It wouldn't scare me now, but it did then. When I woke up I'd forgotten who you were. Pat stuck his head in the door and asked if you were all right." She smiled. "I thought at first that he thought I'd killed you. But he said you have nightmares a lot."

"Wake me if I have another."

"You're not supposed to."

"I'd rather you did."

"All right."

He buttoned his shirt and stood, suddenly anxious to leave.

It was less than half a mile through the woods to Ritter's farm. They emerged from the trees, slid between fence rails and walked through Ritter's pasture. The ponies trotted across the field to meet them, then followed them but would not be petted. Christine walked backward, coaxing them.

Though there was an old cast-iron lawn chair on the front porch, as well as a rocker, Ritter sat on the bottom step of the porch hunched over a magazine and looking curiously like a decrepit yoga. On the concrete walk beneath his feet lay about a dozen ground cigarette butts as well as numerous patches of split. He glanced up as the gate to the pasture squeaked, seemed annoyed at the interruption and turned back to his magazine without nodding.

"This is Christine."

Ritter studied her briefly. "Red hair," he said, then turned to Josh. "I've met them all before. Look at this."

He handed Josh the magazine. The open page contained a picture of four rustic youths squatting in front of a teepee.

"They're not real Indians," he explained. "It's another commune. Out West. Believe in free love. That what you believe in?"

"Not exactly," Josh smiled.

"Why not?" Ritter waited for an answer. "How many of them do you suppose there are?"

"What?"

"Communes!"

"I don't know."

"A lot?"

"More and more."

Ritter nodded and smiled to himself. He seemed to consider himself a part of it all, the article, the commune and all the others of which he had not heard.

"You know them?" he asked.

"No."

"Thought maybe you were all tied together. A kind of club or something."

Josh shook his head.

"Just as well," Ritter muttered, though he was obviously disappointed.

The phone began to ring through the screen door at short, annoying intervals. Ritter sat perfectly still as if mesmerized by its repetition. Christine, assuming that he was hard of hearing, told him that it was ringing.

"I hear it!" he snapped.

They listened impatiently as it continued, wondering if the old man's joints had stiffened in his crouch so that it was now too painful for him to rise.

"Do you want me to get it?"

Ritter's small, dark eyes darted at Josh. He stood, shuffled slowly up the steps and through the door. The ringing stopped. Ritter reappeared with the phone in his hand. He eased himself down the steps, sat and placed the phone beside him. Josh's eyes followed the length of cord to the point where it had been ripped from the wall. He looked at Ritter incredulously.

"Easier to answer out here," Ritter explained, poker-faced, as though what he had done was quite natural.

They wondered whether the old man had gone crazy. Then it occurred to Josh who the phone call had been from. Christine stood close to him.

"Why did you do that?"

"Easier. Not so far to walk."

"Have people been bothering you because of us?"

"No."

"They have."

"No bother. Gives me a chance to talk to people I haven't seen since the last time I told them what I thought of them. Especially the women, you know, I like to tell them to piss in their pants. It gets them so choked up that it's hard to hang up before they do." He glanced at Christine. "No offense.

"Now it's just the same people calling again. Get tired of it after a while." He nodded toward the phone.

"What do they want?"

"Want me to throw you off. They say if I do, they'll see you don't find any place else."

"Who?"

"Everybody. Nobody you know."

"Why?"

"They're just scared. They get scared of things they can't figure out. Then if they're scared long enough they start hating them. That's the only way they manage to stay on top." He eyed them skeptically to see if they followed and fully savored his insight. Then he cleared his throat and spat upon the walk.

"Why don't they come to *us*?"

"They don't know you," Ritter grinned. He and Josh studied one another.

"Do you want us to leave?"

"You'll stay," Ritter said simply. "Just mind your own business and it'll pass. Any more trouble?"

"Kids drive by now and then and yell at us, or force us off the road when we're walking. They throw beer bottles sometimes, but that doesn't matter as long as they keep going. There hasn't been any real trouble."

"There were some people spying on us last night," said Christine.

"I heard about that. Three calls. If you're going to do that stuff in the open you ought to charge admission."

Christine blushed, wondering how much the story had changed by the time it got to him and what else they might have seen.

"How's your money?" Ritter asked. "You're not going hungry, are you?"

"Pat and I still have a lot left."

"I have some in the bank," Christine added.

"I owe you fifty, don't I? I lose track. Got to remind me."

Ritter went inside and returned with fifty dollars in cash. Josh met him at the door.

"You need a rifle?" he asked Josh quietly.

"No."

"I don't think you'll need one, but if you do, just ask."

He looked at Christine who had remained in the yard and was staring across the road at the orchard.

"Pretty, aren't they, when the blossoms come out?" he asked her.

"They're beautiful. They're like pink snow."

Ritter nodded, then coughed and began to wheeze. The sound, barely audible, was like that of another living thing inside his chest. He turned and went inside without saying goodbye, but when they reached the road he came back to the door and watched them until they were out of sight.

Chapter Nine

A month passed, and spring passed into early summer. Every morning Josh would wake before Christine or any of the others and dress quietly in order not to wake her. He would look at her face half hidden behind her disheveled hair and at her shape always curled beneath the covers, then he would slip out the door. He would stand on the porch and watch the sunlight sweep across the hills and change them from gray to deep green or watch the dew rise in plateaus from the valleys and hover above the woods like smoke from a smoldering fire. Eventually the deer found the salt lick he had placed in the orchard. They came late at night when the windows were no longer lighted and the house was silent, but a few occasionally remained past dawn. He would watch them, then walk toward them. They would stare at the house until they distinguished his figure, look at one another, then race down the hill out of sight.

Gradually they let him come closer but never as near as had the doe in the headlights.

On mornings when it was raining, he would watch the rain beat on the barn roof and the road or watch the wind-rolled fog slip along the aisles between apple trees as if fleeing, as the dense, gray daylight swelled. He would walk shirtless in either the rain or the sunlight between the short, green rows of vegetables, measuring their growth by how nearly they came to his knees. Each day he had difficulty detecting a change, then suddenly, after perhaps a week, he would realize how quickly things had grown.

Nearly always, in her sleep, Christine would sense that he was gone. She would wake knowing where he was, then slip into a white fur bathrobe that was the only remnant of a world that she had left. It hung nearly to the floor and seemed too large for her; its hem gathered dust each time she bent over. Its large, fluffy collar nearly concealed her completely and made her appear smaller and younger than she was.

Whether or not it was raining, she would lean out the window and watch him walking between rows of corn, staring at them as if he expected them to grow before his eyes. It was as if everything he believed in or hoped for lay in the field, as if he looked to the plants each morning for the measure of the success of the commune.

Sensing that she was watching him, he would turn toward the window, then walk toward the house, glancing at least once over his shoulder at the field. He would stand beneath the window strumming an imaginary guitar, or move his lips and extend his arms as though he were singing her an aria. Then he would raise the ladder and climb up to their window. On the few mornings that she did not wake, he would rap gently on the window, press his nose against it and make faces as she sat up in bed. She would walk naked to the window as he opened it, laugh as he grabbed her hips and stuck the tip of his tongue into her navel, and duck away as he reached for her breasts.

He would climb through the window and they would make love in the early morning, for it seemed to hold more privacy than the night. After they had made love he would sometimes fall asleep again lying between her legs, with his head on her belly rising and falling with her breath.

One morning at breakfast, Maureen announced that she was pregnant, and Mike added that, for the hell of it, they had decided to get married. A pall of silence hung over the table until Maureen explained that she wanted to have a baby; then there were congratulations. They talked about what it would be like to have children on the farm. Everyone enjoyed the idea, and a few talked about writing friends who had children and inviting them to join. Cyndee had a friend named Alice who lived alone in the East Village with her illegitimate baby boy. She decided to write to her that morning.

Mike and Maureen visited an elderly justice of the peace who was also a retired dairy farmer. He told them that he was bound by law to marry them, and would, but that he considered a marriage profane and hollow unless performed by an ordained minister. Josh's old Nash, Mike's relatively short hair and Maureen's simplicity led him to assume that they were a typical young couple who had run away to elope. When the hearse pulled in the driveway the following morning, and everyone piled out, he and his wife knew immediately who they were and stood in the doorway, open-mouthed, staring with a mixture of awe and dread. Both of them were dressed in their Sunday best, and the house was spotless, but only the old man was angered by the fact that no one but Mike and Maureen had bothered to change out of his workshirt and jeans for the occasion. He was angered, too, because he felt that he had been duped.

He performed the ceremony hurriedly and without a trace of emotion, while his small, gray wife sat at the dining room table filling out the marriage certificate and a large card entitled Rememberances of Our Wedding Day that she had purchased especially for them; it had a woman in a full-length gown and a man in evening dress on its cover.

The old man toyed with a wart on his knuckle while Mike and Maureen kissed, then stared as if admonishing them to leave. His wife, however, had decided very quickly that they were polite young people who had merely gone slightly astray. She told them to make themselves at home while she made punch and prepared a tray of cookies. When her husband tried to intervene, she shot him a reproving glance to remind him that it *was* a wedding. He strode deliberately up the stairs, began pacing the floor above them and did not show his face again. When the punch and cookies were gone, she nodded goodbye to each of them as they thanked her, then stood on the porch with a fleeting, nervous smile and waved as they drove away with Mike and Maureen sitting regally upon the roof of the hearse.

As they passed through the town Pat blew the horn

while Maureen smiled and waved, taking dandelions from a bouquet they had presented to her and casting them at the occasional pedestrian, who regarded them dispassionately or with outright contempt. When they arrived back at the farm they sat on the porch passing around bottles of apple wine and devouring a rich chocolate cake that Cyndee had laced heavily with grass. Pat handed Mike two capsules wrapped in aluminum foil.

"What are they?"

"Honeymoon pills," Pat grinned. "A present from the Apple Gods."

Mike and Maureen washed the pills down with wine from a large red vase. A half-hour later, their cheeks puffed and made childlike by the drug, they disappeared hand in hand into the orchard. Pat, smoking a cigar he had bought especially for the occasion, stared after them, then grinned at Josh and Christine.

"Yes, sir. Only the best for my kids."

Christine, with her arm around Josh, noted traces of sincere affection beneath his mimicry and liked him for the first time. Yet it seemed to her that her smile made him wince. He nodded, then turned with the cigar in his mouth and his hands in his pockets and walked by himself toward the woods.

It was not until early July that the hostility they thought had begun to wane began coming to a head. Bickford drove up the mountain road one afternoon, parked the car and stared up at the farmhouse. He strode slowly up the porch and knocked upon the screen door. Cyndee answered it and was surprised to see a stranger. She invited him inside; he thanked her and self-consciously returned her smile but explained that he was looking for Josh. She pointed toward the orchard and stared after him as he left, nervously chewing her lip and wondering whether she had done the right thing; Rodney was paranoic about the F.B.I. and there had always been speculation as to whether Josh and Pat might have actually deserted from the army.

Josh was limbing a felled, dead tree while Pat and Peter swayed back and forth with a cross saw dividing its trunk into chunks. He glanced up from his work and, for a moment, did not recognize Bickford, then smiled and greeted him. Pat and Peter stopped working and stared at him curiously. Bickford nodded to them shyly while Josh explained that it was he who had helped him find the farm. He apologized to Bickford for not having stopped back to thank him, explaining how busy they had been. Bickford complimented him on the transformation of the farm, adding that he had guessed that Josh and Ritter would get along. Then his mood appeared abruptly to change and he asked quietly if he could speak to Josh alone.

The two of them walked uphill through the orchard toward the road. Bickford's shoulders were stooped, and his hands in the pockets of his khaki pants appeared to be groping for words. Josh waited for him to speak then guessed what he was trying to say.

"Did they send you to tell us to leave?"

"No," Bickford answered quietly. "I wouldn't do that."

"There's trouble, though, isn't there?"

"There was a meeting last night. About twenty-five people got together to decide what to do about you."

"What did they decide?"

"That they couldn't do anything, really, unless they

could get Ritter on their side. And they've about given up on him. Most of them figured that you probably wouldn't be able to make it through the winter and thought they might as well wait and see."

"Is that all?"

"Not exactly. They've decided not to sell you anything, any food or gas or anything like that." Bickford smiled. "Everyone went for the idea except Samuel Fletcher. He went for it, too, after they accused him of worrying about his profits."

Bickford explained that this was all that had been decided, but that a few people had remained dissatisfied when they left and had begun talking among themselves.

"I didn't say anything because I knew it wouldn't do any good. The minute I open my mouth I'm an outsider. I thought it would be better just to listen and let you know what happened."

Josh thanked him. They stood at the road. Bickford was obviously anxious to leave before a car passed and someone saw him associating with the commune. He told Josh that it would be better if he did not come to visit him or his daughter. Then he asked him not to tell anyone that he knew him and had helped him find the farm, explaining that he could find out more if no one knew these things. Josh saw that Bickford was frightened and realized that this was his real motivation for coming.

Bickford, knowing that Josh understood, could not look at him as he wished him luck. Josh nodded and forced a smile but did not thank him again as he left.

"What'd he want?" asked Pat, who had followed him up to the road.

"Fletcher's not going to sell us anything."

"Where you going?"

"Fletcher's."

Pat, grinning and ready for a fight, climbed into the car beside him. When they passed a truck that nearly forced them off the mountain road, he leaned out the window and cursed its driver, then riddled it with bullets from an imaginary machine gun.

Fletcher, nervous and frightened, braced himself as they walked into the store. Josh crossed directly to him and stood before him at the counter.

"I can't sell you anything."

"Why?" Josh asked calmly.

"That's my business."

"I'd just like to know."

"You don't belong around here. If it was one or two of you, we might let it go. But not a whole houseful."

"Let it go? Let it go! That's white of you!" Pat exclaimed. Grinning sardonically he made a formal bow toward Fletcher. "Your generosity is overwhelming."

"What have we done to you?" Josh asked.

Fletcher's chalk-white face flushed, his eyes narrowed. He leaned over the counter with renewed courage and confidence, glaring at Josh.

"Look at you! You look like a zoo!"

"What does it matter what we look like?"

"There are girls! How many of them are married? We've got kids, a lot of us. We know what you are. It's not as if you're trying to hide it."

"What are we?"

Fletcher, breathing deeply to control himself, leaned farther toward them with his long white fingers spread upon the counter.

"Pigs," he whispered. "Pigs!"

"Christ," Pat muttered to himself. He frowned and, for a moment, stared sadly at the floor. "Kill the pigs kill the pigs kill the pigs." Then he stared at Fletcher viciously and grinned. "You wouldn't know a pig if it went to bed with you!"

"Get out of here," Fletcher ordered, "or I'll call the police."

Pat, nearly a foot shorter, walked up to him and met his eyes.

"Listen, you son of a bitch, you don't even know what the law is! It's against the law not to sell to us! Do you know that?"

Fletcher grabbed the receiver of the phone from the wall and held it out threateningly as he warned them.

"If you don't get out of here right now you'll find out what the law is!"

"Come on," Josh said to Pat. Pat ignored him.

He crossed to the refrigerator and ripped a beer out of its cardboard case. He slammed it on the counter.

"How much?"

Fletcher began to dial. Pat tossed a quarter on the counter, picked up the beer and went out the door after Josh. When they were in the car he unscrewed the lid and swallowed half of it in one drink. Then he smirked.

"You're an ass-kissing son of a bitch sometimes. I never told you that, did I?" Josh didn't answer. "What did you come down here for, anyway?"

"To ask him to ask the rest of them to come and meet us."

"Are you serious?"

"Forget it."

"Boy, you really are! What did you think that would accomplish?"

"Forget it!"

"Look, nothing's going to make any difference to them. Play Sir Galahad and they'll just shoot you off your fucking white horse. Shoot your white horse, too, for that matter."

"You don't need to make things worse."

"Worse? How could it be worse? They hate us. Anyway, there's nothing they can do unless we let them, and they know it."

"They can do anything they want to do if enough of them want to do it. They're their laws, not ours."

"The law can't touch us."

"It can if it wants to. Anyway, it doesn't matter whether it can or not. They can do anything they want because the law won't touch *them.*"

"How? Unless we let them."

"How do we stop them?"

"Blow their heads off!"

"And get locked up?"

"It might be worth it." Pat lay back in the seat and thought for a moment. "Sometimes I'd like to blow this fucking country off the earth. You know what I mean?"

"You should have stayed in the army and become a general. You've got a military mentality."

"If I were a general I'd drop a bomb on this town, kill the other fucking generals and blow my own head off, in that order. Anyway, I didn't ask if I had a military mentality; I asked if you knew what I meant."

Josh thought for a moment, then nodded that he did.

Chapter Ten

The following day was the Fourth of July, but no one knew it until Pat, Jerry and Maureen drove to Simpsonville for supplies and found the stores closed. Pat was annoyed, then he remembered posters he had seen on telephone poles in Heartwell advertising an annual Independence Day celebration and an idea occurred to him.

"You're crazy!" Maureen exclaimed. "You really are! Do you *want* to get killed?"

Pat grinned. "We'll be in and out before they know what's hit them."

"Zap!" said Jerry, who immediately took to the prank, managing somehow to see in it a dimension of primitive symbolism. "We'll blow their minds!"

At last Maureen reluctantly agreed. One pharmacy in town had remained open; they purchased bandages, gauze and several bottles of mercurochrome.

Independence Day, Town Meeting day and the three days of the County Fair were perhaps the most important of the year to those living in and around Heartwell, for only on these days did the disparate, rural population pause to recognize and even gloat upon itself as a community. On Independence Day there was always a cookout and an outdoor dance, with fireworks, at which all except the oldest and youngest were too self-conscious to do anything but sit and talk or listen to the music.

The festivities were initiated at noon by a small parade. It was assembling at the outskirts of town by the time Pat and the others returned. There was a high school band. In front of it were three floats. One bore a huge American flag fashioned from wire and artificial flowers made of toilet paper and Kleenex. Another was a flat-bed truck carrying three small children in uniforms posing as the Spirit of '76. Both afraid and anxious to begin, they stood fidgeting atop the truck, one waving a flag, another pretending to blow a fife and the third creating a nervous rhythm on the drum to the consternation of Fletcher, who appeared to be in charge.

On the third float, another flat-bed truck, two men dressed in overalls and bearing muskets posed as though taking pot shots at several of their red-coated friends. There were also several small regiments of veterans of the various wars, including four young men who had fought in Indo-China. Their vanguard was an ancient, somewhat senile man in a wheel chair decorated with flags. He claimed to have fought beside Teddy Roosevelt. There was no one left to dispute him; those who allowed him to lead the march each year did so not because they believed him but because they wanted to believe him, a man with such a history being an asset to the town.

Pat turned onto a dirt road about a quarter mile from where the parade was set to begin. He and Jerry sponged their faces with mecurochrome, poured it over their work shirts and tore them into shreds on their bodies. Maureen wrapped them with bloody looking bandages, drew scars on their faces and arms with a lining pencil then colored the sockets of their eyes black. They worked with determination only occasionally interrupted by fits of laughter as they gaped at one another.

"This is suicide!" Maureen warned them. Grinning nervously they nodded in agreement, yet none of them seemed really to care. They listened to the band begin to play, stood at the edge of the woods near the highway as the parade began making its way toward town.

In an orderly fashion, the hearse glided up behind the Spirit of '76. Pat, red-stained and ragged, lay upon his back on the hood. With his eyes open and blank, his body rigid and absolutely still, his head grotesquely cocked and his tongue hanging from his mouth, his imitation of a corpse cast a momentary pall over the crowd lining the street. Maureen, who drove, sensed as she watched him through the windshield that he did not consider this a joke at all, that he was absolutely serious in what he was doing, and that he was frightened.

The first of the people who stared at Pat were horrified and outraged. Then Maureen stupified them by waving and smiling as though her presence was to be assumed, though she feared that at any moment the hearse would be mobbed. Bumper stickers surrounding the corpse on the hood further confused them. EAT

OUT ... IT'S FUN! the stickers suggested. The crowd recognized these as part of a campaign being waged by the Vermont Diner's Association, and most of them could not rule out the possibility that this organization had had the madness to ask the commune to represent it. A few began to hiss and jeer, but even the police were not sure that this last, bizarre float, was not legitimate.

EAT OUT ... IT'S FUN! the bright yellow stickers reiterated along the side of the hearse.

When the crowd saw Jerry's bloody head and arms, and especially his long hair, dangling out the open door at the rear of the hearse, it was swept up in a second, intense wave of anger. Those on the other floats interrupted their poses to see what was causing the commotion behind them. Then one of the youths who already had a grudge against the commune hurled an empty soft drink can at Jerry. It struck him in the ear; he drew his head inside and slammed the door as the boy started toward him. Pat remained without the slightest change in his pose of death as apple cores and other missiles struck and sailed past him, while Maureen blared the horn and tried to nudge past the floats.

Then a stone smashed one of the passenger windows and a few more of the most militant youths began moving into the street. Pat finally stood and climbed to safety atop the roof, taunting the crowd with his grin, waving to them and clenching his hands above his head, then giving them the sign of peace as Maureen maneuvered past the flat-bed trucks and sped toward the other end of town.

By the time they reached the top of the mountain, a police car, too, had made its way through the crowd and caught up with them. The three of them were ordered to lean against the hearse as they were brusquely searched. Josh and Christine walked out of the farmhouse in time to see them loaded into the police car.

"Police brutality!" Pat shouted to both of them. At a distance, they were momentarily fooled by his mutilated face. Then he shrugged his shoulders, smiled and waved goodbye as they were driven off; Maureen and Jerry, more subdued, glanced back at Josh helplessly.

The rest of the commune pursued them in the Nash and only began to guess what had happened when they saw the floats parked in front of Fletcher's store and as the remnants of the crowd cursed at them and glared. At the county jail in Simpsonville, Josh tried vainly to post bail. Everyone of authority had taken a holiday, or so they were told. The officer in charge would only tell him that they would be brought to court in the morning. He threatened to arrest the rest of them if they did not leave.

The following morning, in a small, austere courtroom in the town hall, they stood before a bald, officious judge and pleaded guilty. He gave them a choice of one-hundred-dollar fines or ten days in jail for disturbing the peace, assuming that they would not have the money to pay the fines, muttering that he would as soon lock them up and throw away the key. When Pat raised one of his boots and took three crisp one-hundred-dollar bills from a secret compartment in the heel, the judge was furious.

"Where did you get that?"

"Blood money," Pat answered simply.

"What?"

"I was a hired killer."

The judge stared at him blankly, not sure whether Pat was crazy, serious or merely playing a game. The court-room attendant watched Pat closely and prepared to restrain him. Josh and Christine seated on wooden benches at the other end of the room, tried to motion Pat to be quiet while other members of the commune merely closed their eyes and shook their heads or low-ered their heads to hide their grins.

"Who did you kill?"

"No one to speak of—a lot of little yellow people."

"You were paid to kill them?" the judge asked care-fully, more convinced now that Pat suffered from an insanity probably attributable to drugs.

"Yes."

"Who paid you?"

"The army." Unabashed, Pat smiled.

The judge breathed deeply. He paused long enough to gather his temper, then glared directly down at Pat.

"Do you know what the maximum sentence for disturbing the peace is?"

Pat shrugged. Jerry and Maureen shook their heads.

"A year!"

"I believe, though, Your Honor, that you missed your chance."

"We'll see! You'll be in here again. I guarantee it." He turned to the guard. "Get them out of here!"

When they were gone the judge conferred quietly with the arresting officers.

On the trip back to the commune no one was willing to joke with Pat about the disturbances he had caused. Josh treated him cooly, explaining how they had been tyrannized throughout the night, how cars had passed repeatedly with their horns blaring; how the same carload of youths Pat had previously antagonized had parked and begun shouting at the house, cursing and trying to goad them into another fight. He told Pat how, before they had finally left, one had hurled a stone that smashed a bedroom window.

"And I suppose you sat there and let them?" Pat asked. He frowned when Josh didn't answer. Sensing that everyone was angry with him, even Jerry and Maureen, he said nothing more.

That evening the commune was raided. There was no warning, no sirens or flashing lights. The State Police, County Sheriff and his deputies merely surrounded the farmhouse and crept up on it after the last lighted window had grown dark. They burst through both doors with their pistols drawn, shouting who they were and that any resistance would be in violation of the law. They threw open bedroom doors before most of them knew what was happening.

A young, crew-cut deputy not much older than Josh broke into his and Christine's room and caught them scrambling into their clothes.

"Get out of here!" Josh screamed.

For a moment the cop seemed self-conscious in his role. Then he was only angry, revolted at the length of Josh's hair.

"Don't tell me where to get! Get dressed right where you are!" Josh eyed him furiously. The cop trained his eyes on Christine. "You two married?"

"None of your business!"

"There's not a law in this state, but there ought to be." He grinned maliciously. "There ought to be. I wish there was."

"Don't point that, please!" Christine begged him. He looked at the pistol he had inadvertantly aimed in her direction, hesitated, then aimed it instead at Josh.

They were herded into the living room and made to sit huddled upon the floor for three hours while the police searched every corner of the house, emptying every drawer upon the floor and pulling every mattress from its frame, taking every picture from the wall, examining every ash tray, every crack in the soft chairs, every open can in the refrigerator and every kitchen cupboard. They studied such unlikely places as the bottom of the toilet seat in the outhouse, growing more embarrassed and thus angrier, more violent and determined in their search as time passed. They found only several plastic containers filled with birth control pills and a prescription of tranquilizers belonging to Rodney, and these they confiscated.

Finally, when they were faced with re-sifting the shambles they had created, they marched into the living room and demanded to know where the drugs were hidden.

"Is *that* what you're looking for?" Pat said to the husky, pock-marked cop who had been one of those to arrest him. "Why didn't you ask us before? It would have saved a lot of trouble." The others looked at him, begging him with their eyes not to give them away.

Surprised at his cooperation and at the same time distrustful, the police waited for him to say more.

"We don't use that awful stuff," Pat explained. "Jumping Jehoshaphat, you think we want to become a bunch of addicts?" he grinned.

The big cop kicked Pat's arms from behind him, stared down as if about to strike him in the face.

"Sit up and shut your mouth!"

"What's your name?" asked another older cop who appeared to be in charge.

"Bazooka Joe." The big cop moved toward him threateningly. Pat smiled apologetically. "That's my nickname. My real name's Pat Depew. It rhymes with Bazooka Joe if you pronounce Joe like Jew."

The big cop kicked him in the thigh before the older cop could order him to stop. When Pat went for the cop, Josh grabbed his arm.

"Shut up," Josh whispered to him. "Just shut up, will you?"

"Let him go!" the big cop said, ready to kick him again.

"Cool off, Max," said another, mellower cop, who seemed only to be bored and to wish he were in bed. "You'll have a heart attack."

Cyndee, noting how late it was asked them if they would like an early breakfast. Furious at having made fools of themselves in front of people they loathed, and realizing there was nothing more they could do, they prepared to leave with the birth control pills and tranquilizers in a metal box that bore an adhesive tape label marked Evidence.

"By the way," Pat said, "have you got a warrant?"

The older, graying cop took a document from his back pocket and held it before him.

"Want to read it?"

"No thanks. We'll take your word."

The big cop lingered as the others walked onto the porch. Staring malevolently at Pat, then the others, he seemed to be groping for words. Finally, he spat deliberately toward them, turned and strode out the door.

Chapter Eleven

Though the police began making irregular patrols of the mountain road, they did not return to the commune. A small wooden chest containing an array of drugs, buried beneath an inch of soil between two rows of corn, was for the most part left untouched during the following weeks.

Alice, a tall girl with a boyish face, close-cropped hair and masculine physique, arrived hitchhiking with her baby boy in a brightly woven sack strapped upon her back. She carried him with her everywhere she went. When she was working in the orchards Horace would be nearby, crawling through the tall grass, chasing and devouring insects. When she was in the field weeding or thinning the crop he lay beside her, eating dirt or small string beans that she picked for him. Often he would merely sit absolutely still and watch her.

Alice had given birth to him with only the help of a friend in a dingy, two-room apartment in the Lower

East Side. She had done so in order to be certain that there would be no official record of his birth. She believed that Horace, a numberless, legal nonentity possessed a freedom that was stolen from the hordes of children who were tagged, filed and footprinted the moment they slid into the world. Indeed, she believed that Horace was one of the very few free human beings left.

He was a contented child and rarely cried except when he was hungry. During the evenings and early mornings someone was always in the front yard or on the living room floor playing with him. At the dinner table he would often hurl food at Pat, who led him on. Everyone enjoyed having him; he seemed to symbolize the permanence of the commune.

Josh paid frequent visits to Ritter, sometimes with Christine, whose company the old man had grown to enjoy. Two cords of wood had been stacked beside his barn; on the cooler summer nights when they would knock at his door, he would build a fire. They would sit around it, and Ritter would listen, always more patient at night than during the day, while Josh told him how the commune was progressing and about any new plans they might have made.

Occasionally Ritter would talk about the past, of harsh winters and work horses that pulled giant cylinders that packed the snow on the road instead of plowing it, that passed so quietly on winter mornings that one could only hear the horses' snorting and the rattling and rubbing of harnesses. They learned that he had once been married, but were not told whether his wife had died or left. They learned, also, that he had had children and had sent them away to college where the only thing they learned was that they didn't want to live on a farm. When asked where his children had gone, he said simply that they were somewhere waiting for him to die so that they could inherit and sell his land. He grinned as he said it; neither Josh nor Christine could tell whether he was serious.

Often when he spoke he would stare shamelessly at Christine's breasts beneath her workshirt, fascinated by pointed nipples where he was accustomed to seeing the blunt, disappointing shape of a brassiere. He was always asking whether there had been trouble. Josh always replied that there had been none. When he learned of the prank Pat had pulled during the parade, he was angry that no one had told him and, most of all, because he had not been there to observe and relish the reaction of the town.

No one knew who told Ritter about the embargo placed upon the commune by the villagers. Perhaps he learned directly from Fletcher, or perhaps he began to wonder and had sought out the answer to why Josh no longer offered him a ride to town. One morning he pulled up in front of the farm in his battered, green pickup truck and asked for Josh. Maureen told him that he was in the field.

"Get him!"

Warned that Ritter was in a foul mood, Josh hurried toward the road.

"Get in!"

"Where are we going?"

"Get in!"

Josh climbed into the truck and stared at Ritter, waiting for an explanation. Ritter, hunched over the wheel in his dusty, double-breasted suitcoat and breathing asthmatically, glared angrily at the road.

"What's wrong?"

Ritter's eyes darted at him. He said nothing.

"Where are we going? I'm just curious." Josh smiled, leaning back with his head bouncing upon the seat. He knew Ritter well enough to know that the old man was not mad at him.

"To buy groceries."

"It'll only cause trouble. It's not worth it."

"He can't do it, unless you let him. It's against the law. Even I know that."

"The law doesn't make any difference."

"We'll see if it does."

"I didn't tell you we were raided the other night."

"You didn't tell me anything!" Ritter snapped. "What do you mean, raided?"

"The police broke in, herded us up like cattle and tore the house apart."

"You *let* them?"

"How are we supposed to *stop* them? Who are we supposed to call, the *police?*"

Ritter grunted, then had to slow the truck nearly to a stop as he began coughing uncontrollably. Josh was afraid that the old man would have a heart attack or that the wheezing, living thing inside him would choose this moment to cut off his breath.

"Did they find anything?" he asked at last.

"No."

"Sue them!"

"Sue *who?*" Josh asked. "Don't you see? The only thing to do is leave it alone. They'll forget about us after a while."

"You *believe* that?"

"You said it yourself."

"I didn't think you were going to let them walk all over you! They'll do that as long as you let them."

"Maybe not. Maybe not fighting is the only way to get people to leave you alone."

"Botch!" Ritter rasped. "Claptrap! Who taught you to think like that?"

"Nobody," Josh shrugged. "Anyway, I said maybe."

"That's the kind of stuff that will get you killed. That's all it's good for."

"Even if it is, it's up to us, not you. It's not going to do any good to make them hate you, too."

"Hate! They don't *hate* me. They haven't got enough *sense!* You can't hate someone if you think he's crazy. That's why it pays to let people think you're nuts!" he grinned.

It was Saturday afternoon. People were sitting on their porches or working in their yards. They glanced up as Ritter's truck passed. As it parked in front of the store, they stopped what they were doing and watched. Ritter shuffled into the store ahead of Josh.

"We've come to shop. What's your special?"

Fletcher avoided Ritter's eyes and walked out from behind the counter, away from him.

"I won't sell to him. You know that."

"I don't know anything! All I want to know is what's your special. Cabbage? Squash?" Ritter grinned at Josh. "Got to be careful of his specials. Usually only means the stuff is rotten."

Fletcher turned on him angrily. "Listen! Don't push me! You get him out of here or I'll call the state police!"

"Forget it!" Josh pleaded to Ritter. "It doesn't matter!" He was ashamed at letting the old man fight for him and felt like a child helplessly caught between arguing adults.

"The police!" Ritter snapped. "That'd be Max Paxton and Randy Childs!" He leaned over the counter but could not reach the phone. "Give it to me! I'll call them myself!"

"Go ahead, but they'll arrest him for trespassing if I tell them to. Max Paxton would as soon shoot this boy as look at him. Did you know his younger brother was killed in the war two months ago?"

"What's that got to do with it?" Josh asked.

"Everything! He didn't die so that you could run around tearing down everything he fought for! So that you could run around making fools of us all!"

"What *did* he die for?"

Fletcher and Josh looked at one another for a moment, then Fletcher reached for the phone.

"I'm leaving," Josh said to Ritter. "Let it go. Please."

"Wait a minute!" Ritter snapped, but Josh had turned and gone out the screen door. "You going to stop selling to me, too?" he asked Fletcher bitterly.

"Buy what you want, but keep him out of here."

Ritter smiled coyly. "All right, I think I can guess what they need." He tossed a sack of potatoes on the counter then grabbed an armload of cans. "These eggs from Jordan's hens?"

"Don't push me," Fletcher said quietly.

"Are they or aren't they?"

"Yes."

"I'll take them anyway."

"If you start pushing, people will start pushing back."

"Don't talk to me about pushing! Don't talk at all!"

Ritter took a paper bag from beneath the counter and helped himself to a dozen eggs. Outside he heard a car pass and several youths shouting.

"Ring it up!" he ordered, then leaned against the counter in a fit of coughing. When Fletcher made no move, Ritter grabbed a pen and added the figures himself, then threw eight dollars upon the counter. "Keep the change. Do you bag them or do I?"

Fletcher eyed Ritter coldly, then reached for a paper bag. When it was full Ritter grabbed it along with the bag of eggs and started for the door. The cash register rang.

Fletcher slapped the change upon the counter.

"Keep it!" Ritter rasped. "Buy yourself a cigar!"

Josh, who had been waiting beside the truck, took the larger bag from Ritter and opened the door. Ritter grinned at him triumphantly, but they did not speak to one another. A run-down, two-tone Chevrolet roared down the road toward them. It slowed and the big youth behind the wheel, the one who had climbed the ladder after Pat, leaned out the window to shout at Josh. Ritter reached into his bag, pulled out two eggs and hurled them. One smashed and slid across the hood. The second exploded just below the boy's ear. He screamed as though he had been shot.

Ritter, surprised at the accuracy of his awkward throw, roared with laughter. The car's tires squealed and its doors flew open. The two boys started for Ritter, then stopped as if it had suddenly occured to them that he was an old man. Josh dropped the groceries and stepped between Ritter and the boys. He and the big boy recognized one another. The younger, smaller boy had the same square, flat features but also possessed the heavy jaw and listless eyes of the slow-witted.

They stared at Josh as though prepared to kill him, but made no move. Another carload of boys drove up from the opposite direction and lept out to watch. A small group of men and children gathered across the street. Then Ritter shuffled up beside Josh, still snickering at the mixture of yoke and shell dripping from the side of the big boy's head.

"You sure are a messy eater. Didn't anyone ever tell you not to swallow through your ear?" Ritter gasped and doubled up with laughter. Henry wiped his ear with the sleeve of his shirt. His eyes darted between Ritter and Josh. Josh, with his hands in his hip pockets, merely stared at him, waiting for a fight.

"You'd better get him out of here!"

"Don't you tell me what to do!" Ritter snapped. He turned to Josh. "This is Henry Mason and his brother Cal. Their father used to mow the orchard every summer. Henry. Cal. This is Josh." Josh stared through them at the crowd gathering near the curb. "And that's Jim Potter, the big one with the beer belly. And Bill and Bobby Hatchett, and Gary Carruthers. Nice weather," he nodded and said to them.

"Kick the shit out of him! What are you waiting for?" shouted one of the carload of boys. All of them were impatient for the fight to begin.

Henry had the edge on Josh in weight but not in height; he obviously did not want a fight. Each time the boys goaded him, he clenched his fists but hesitated before taking a step; his eyes wavered nervously.

"Wait a minute!" said Potter. "You come over here, Cal, so it will be even. Henry can handle it."

Cal asked his brother if it was all right. Henry did not answer.

"Come on, Cal."

Cal walked to the curb, relieved to be out of it and

suddenly more anxious to see the fight begin. Ritter, who had finally realized how serious the situation was, tried to intervene.

"You'll fight me, if anybody," he said to Henry. "I'm the one who threw it."

"Stay out of this! It's fair enough!" Potter exclaimed, gesticulating with his pale, fat arms.

Potter had worked up a sweat running merely from his porch to the curb. As he spoke he took a dirty handkerchief from the pocket of his short-sleeve shirt and wiped his face. Then he ran his fingers over his scalp brushing back long strands of straight hair that were meant to cover a bald spot atop his head. "What about it, boy?" he shouted to Josh. "It's fair enough, isn't it?"

Josh's eyes darted past Henry at Potter. As they glared at one another, Potter's lips formed a barely detectable grin.

"I don't want to fight you," Josh said to Henry. He turned away from him and walked toward the bag he had left on the ground.

The other carload of boys whispered loudly, "Get him!"

"You going to let him go?"

Goaded and suddenly seeing an advantage, Henry went for Josh. Josh heard him, spun and kicked him in the groin. Henry collapsed, moaning and writhing on the pavement. From the force of the kick Josh, too, lost his balance and fell. Cal started across the road but stopped the moment Josh was up again. Potter, his round face shining with sweat, glowered at him.

"That's not fair!" he yelled. That's dirty fighting!"

"Botch!" Ritter shouted back. He was elated by the way Josh had handled it.

"I don't want to fight you," Josh said again to Henry. "Just leave us alone."

Potter trotted across the road and knelt over the boy to help him. But Henry, still curled on his side and gasping for breath, begged to be left alone. Finally, Potter looked up at Josh and snarled.

"For two cents I'd whip you so you couldn't walk."

Josh looked directly at him. He licked his lips as though trying to hold back his words then whispered so that no one else could hear. "Try it. I'd just love you to try it."

Potter's eyes wavered. He pretended to focus his attention on Henry again until Josh had turned away. Josh picked up the bag of groceries and climbed into the truck, waited for Ritter, then drove away, swerving a-round the cars that had stopped in the road. A stone thrown by one of the boys cracked the back window. Josh pressed the gas pedal to the floor until he reached the mountain road. When he slowed the truck and relaxed his grip after turning, Ritter saw his hands trembling on the wheel. Ritter grinned at him, more impressed by the swiftness and accuracy of his kick than by the way he himself had thrown the egg.

"Where did you learn to fight like that?"

"The army. Hand-to-hand combat."

"Hand-to-hand?" Ritter snickered. "I hope he hasn't got a girl friend. Hand to hand is all he'll be doing for a while."

Josh stared into the rear-view mirror to make sure they were not being followed. He said nothing more and felt oppressed by Ritter's laughter.

Chapter Twelve

Word spread quickly through the community that one of the youths from the commune had come to Fletcher's store and started trouble. Jim Potter called Ralph Mason, and together they phoned the rest of the people in and near the town.

Potter, who owned a shoe store in Simpsonville ten miles away, was not popular with his neighbors. They disliked him because he was overbearing and because his shoes were overpriced and of a low quality. Some of the older members of the community remembered how Potter's father had swindled a popular local farmer out of seventy-five acres of land and held this against the son now that the father was no longer living. The women of the town disliked him most of all because he beat not only his sons but his daughters with a leather belt.

Nearly everyone, however, agreed to attend the meeting that Potter called for that evening. Most of those who came did so out of curiosity rather than anger or a resolve to take action, for they had heard more and more outlandish stories about the life-style of the youths atop the mountain. They had learned, for instance, that boys and girls swam naked together. They had heard that everyone on the commune was married to everyone else, and that only two of them were married legally. They had been told by their sons, who often spied on the farm from the woods at night, that primitive rites were held around fires in which people went naked and painted one another's bodies. There were a few who even believed and confided to one another that the members of the commune held Ritter under an evil spell.

The meeting, held in the town hall, was attended by about twenty men and five women. Youths under the age of twenty-one were not admitted. Potter took the floor immediately. No one was either willing or able to dispute the charge that Josh had been looking for trouble and that he had thrown the egg. Everyone agreed that the members of the commune were pushing their luck, even those who considered the incident humorous.

"We've been through this before," Fletcher said impatiently. "There's nothing we can do so what's the point in talking about it?" Fletcher despised Potter with whom, for many years, he had been waging a subtle battle for the leadership of the town.

Max Paxton, out of uniform, stood like a sentry at the back of the room with his arms crossed. He was the one who had had the confrontation with Pat the night of the raid on the farm. He was tall and, save for a slight paunch, retained an excellent physique he had acquired during eight years of service in the marines. He had had a severe case of acne as an adolescent; the pock marks marred what would have otherwise been a ruddy, handsome face.

"If you'd called me I could have had him arrested for assault." He turned to Mason, the father of the two boys. "I'll have him locked up in the morning if you want to swear out a complaint for Henry."

"I don't!" Mason snapped. "Henry will take care of it himself." He had been furious with his son and ashamed of him upon learning of his reluctance to fight and the abrupt and ignoble way in which he had allowed himself to be defeated. A small, balding man with a round, pleasant face, he sat in the corner brooding beside his wife.

"If you won't press charges, there's nothing we can do. We've tried the only other angle we could come up with. We'll try it again, maybe, but not until we're sure we'll catch them off guard.'

"There are other ways," said Potter.

"If that's what you're going to talk about I'd better leave." Paxton started for the door.

"That's *not* what we're going to talk about," Fletcher answered sharply with his eyes trained upon Potter. He was strictly opposed to acting outside the law and angered at the thought that this might be why Potter had called the meeting.

"Wait a minute," said Potter. "Are there any other legal ways we haven't tried?"

Roberta Sheldon, the wizened, elderly town clerk stood and spoke, glancing at a tattered notebook that she always carried with her.

"There's no way to have Ritter committed. We know that. And there's nothing in zoning that says the group of them can't live there, though we might be able to put something about multiple-family dwellings on the ballot come fall or spring. As a matter of fact," she grinned, "there's nothing to keep them from voting, those that are old enough."

"If we could get their names," Fletcher said to Paxton, "you could find out whether any of them had records."

"It wouldn't matter if they did," Paxton reminded him. "Anyway, we've gotten three of their names and run them through and haven't come up with anything."

"Maybe some of them are draft dodgers," Roberta Sheldon announced, "or are wanted for something else."

Potter interrupted them. "Wait a minute. I might have something." He addressed himself toward the rear left corner of the room, where Bickford was sitting. "My daughter came home from school a few days ago—"

"Good for her," muttered one of the older natives who was thoroughly bored by the proceedings. There was general laughter.

"I'm talking to Bill!" Potter frowned. "She came home and said your daughter had told her a secret. She said she'd tell it to me, too, if I didn't tell anyone else."

"Then I suggest you keep your word," said Fletcher sarcastically. The others, however, were more attentive.

"Do you know what I'm talking about?" Potter asked Bickford.

Bickford nodded, pale and expressionless but trying to maintain his composure. "I know the boy. He stopped in asking about a place to live when he first came here. I fed him breakfast, that's all."

"That's all right, if that's the kind of person you want

to take in. But she also said you led the boy to Ritter. Is that true?" The group turned and regarded Bickford, who nodded.

"Why?" someone asked.

"We won't even ask why. We'll try to assume that's your business too. But there's one other thing." Potter waited, studying Bickford's reaction.

"Come on," Fletcher told him. "We don't need any of this sort of dramatics."

"Julie said your daughter said he had blood all over him when she found him from a deer he'd hit and carried off the road."

"He didn't hit the deer. He found it. He told me about it."

"What makes you think he didn't hit it."

"He said he found it."

"He *said!* He *said* he'd found it?" Potter exclaimed. He paced back and forth across the front of the room, sweating profusely.

"I believe him," Bickford added quietly, mildly belligerent.

"Okay! All right! Let's say he didn't hit it. It'd be hard to prove that he did. Isn't there still a law about finding a dead deer and not reporting it?"

"There is," replied Jack Ferguson, the young and serious-minded game warden. "But it's a little late to do anything about it now. Besides, I don't think we could give him anything more than a fine."

It was a warm, humid summer night. The room had filled with cigar and cigarette smoke. People wiped their faces with handkerchiefs and shirt sleeves. Most were bored and believed already that the meeting was a waste of time. They were annoyed with Potter for having called them, and revealed their impatience with yawns and frowns.

"Okay! All right!" Potter barked. "But suppose that blood wasn't from a deer?"

The room grew silent. Potter glanced over them, smiling.

"That's pretty far flung," Fletcher answered dryly.

"I know it is!" said Potter. "I probably shouldn't even bring it up. But I know one thing. I know by looking at them that most of them aren't right in the head."

"I've heard some stories about them that would make your hair curl," said Roberta Sheldon. Others nodded.

"Exactly. Some of the things that go on up there—you've heard about them. Their *religious meetings.*"

"It's still far flung."

"Besides," Paxton added, "nobody around here has been murdered."

"It wouldn't have had to happen around here. He was coming from somewhere else."

"It wouldn't," muttered someone else. Roberta Sheldon fastened one of her arthritic hands to her throat.

Potter continued. "Any of you remember reading about that group in California? The one that they found had been sacrificing all those human victims?" Some of them nodded. "Well, I'm just saying it's possible. It's the same kind of place and the same kind of people, and we'd just be closing our eyes if we tried to pretend that it wasn't."

"Those kids aren't murderers!" Bickford exclaimed. "They're farmers. Or they want to be if you'll let them alone!"

"Farmers!" Mason exploded bitterly. "Now there's a good one!" Several men laughed.

"All right. Okay," Potter added quietly. "Are there any other possiblities? Any other places that blood might have come from?"

"From a deer!" Bickford answered.

"Did you see the deer?"

"No."

"Your daughter found him, didn't she, passed out in his car? How long was it before she brought him home?"

"What are you getting at?"

"How long?"

"Only a minute."

"How do you know?"

"I know!"

"Couldn't it be just possible that the blood came from your girl."

"No! He didn't hurt her!"

"There are different kinds of blood."

"He didn't touch her! Why are you doing this?" Bickford was shaken and felt trapped within himself as the others stared at him.

"Cut it out, John," Fletcher said angrily. "There's no excuse for even talking like that!" Others, however, were engrossed by these possibilities and acted them out in their imaginations as they waited for Potter to say more.

"Everybody knows," Potter added, "that she's got a way of picking up strangers."

"She's eight years old!"

"Does that make it better or worse?"

Bickford stood, his hands trembling. Then he whispered threateningly and loudly enough so that everyone could hear. "You filthy bastard! Filthy bastard! Don't you mention her again!" His words and even his anger appeared alien to him; it was as if he was suddenly possessed.

"All right. Just one more thing. And I'm not asking you this. I'm asking everybody else. How come you didn't tell anyone you knew the boy and that he'd come to your place. Were you trying to hide something, maybe, something that happened?"

"No!"

"Just maybe." Potter looked at the others, who were entranced.

"No!" Bickford, near tears, started down the aisle toward Potter. Max Paxton and two others restrained him.

"Just maybe something happened that you're a-shamed of and don't want us to know."

"You're sick!" Bickford screamed. "Let go of me! Let go!" He surged out of the hall; the heavy wooden door slammed open against the outside wall.

"We all know who's sick!" Potter yelled after him. "We know who the perverts are around here! The ones that go around looking like girls!"

Bickford sat in his car, his head shaking involuntarily in disbelief of what Potter had done. He did not own a gun. It occurred to him that if he had one, if he were carrying one in his car as did so many of the others, he could take it and murder Potter where he stood. As he cried, he could see himself doing it, emptying a shot gun into the fat man's belly without the slightest remorse.

Suddenly, he was overcome by an irrational dread for his daughter, whom he had left at home alone. He fumbled frantically with the key before starting the car, then he raced out of town.

113

Max Paxton told the audience that he would try to get the name of the boy who had caused the trouble and the rest of the members of the commune and run them through the F.B.I. It was at least possible that some of them might be wanted. Roberta Sheldon asked him to see if there was a law against desecrating a hearse. Paxton said that he would but that he doubted that he would come up with anything.

Nothing more was accomplished at the meeting. Most of the crowd left the town hall disliking Potter even more than they had before, yet few were sorry they had come for it had turned out to be one of the more interesting evenings any of them had known. Though they nearly all agreed with Fletcher that Potter's ideas were far-fetched, he had at the same time helped to crystallize the reasons for their fear. Admitting that a murder or rape committed by members of the commune was at least a possibility, they returned to their homes, knowing nothing except that the commune could not be allowed to remain.

While the meeting had been in progress, and long after it was over, about a dozen youths who had been turned away at the town hall, including Henry and Cal, were gathered at the end of a dead-end dirt road where they often met on Saturday nights when the weather was warm. They sat on the hoods of their dilapidated trucks and cars, drinking beer, wincing and braying, unable to hide their disgust for the bottle of bourbon which they passed around. They sipped it through a plastic straw because they believed that this helped them to get drunk more quickly. They talked more quietly than usual.

Josh and Christine sat on the front porch overlooking

114

the mountains as the last starlike speck from a farm-house window miles away disappeared. A jet passed miles above them; its roar descended in vague, uneven waves. Inside the house Jerry and Alice, who now shared his room, were the only others still awake. They sat on the tattered couch in lamplight listening to Indian music from a battery-powered record player. Christine nodded toward the starlit horizon.

"You can see how the earth is round," she said, "if you look down at it long enough."

Josh nodded. "Sometimes I think I can feel the earth spinning from up here. Do you know? It's the same feeling you get when you're flying in a dream." He walked down into the yard, then turned to her. "Come here."

He watched her walk toward him in a faded pair of jeans, wearing one of his old work shirts with cut-off sleeves. Her hair hung even further than when he had met her and was no longer evenly trimmed. She moved differently, more simply, as though she had lost a shy-ness or conceit she had once held for her own body. Her face was ruddier, more deeply tanned than it had ever been; barely illumined by starlight, it appeared even darker.

"Lie on your back."

"Why?"

He grinned maliciously and toyed with an imaginary moustache.

"Not here!"

He laughed. "Just lie on your back. Don't ask questions."

She lay on her back in the tall grass, looking up at him doubtfully.

"Okay. Now look straight up at the stars. Make sure

you can't see anything else. Use your hands as a visor if you have to."

"You're crazy!"

"Come on! Do it! And when you just see stars concentrate on them until you don't feel as if you're lying on the ground. Until you feel as if you're a star, floating. Tell me when you've got it. Don't hurry."

Josh paced nervously with his hands in his pockets, out of her line of vision.

"Got it?"

"Yes."

"Okay."

He lay beside her so that their bodies touched, and cupped his hands on either side of his face. Together they looked like spectators at a horse race holding imaginary binoculars. A car roared up the road and past the farmhouse, but they were hidden from its headlights.

"Don't laugh. Stars don't laugh," he told her. "Okay. I've got it too. Now lower your left hand to your waist, and I'll lower my right. But make sure you keep seeing only stars."

She slid her hand to her waist. He took it in his own and squeezed it.

"We're stars, and there's nothing around us but stars. If we looked behind us we'd see stars, not earth."

"We'd see the earth too, but it would only be a star."

"Right! We're two stars floating around and holding hands. For stars, holding hands is intercourse. So we're two stars making love."

"I love you."

"Shh! Stars can't say that. They have an alphabet of sunrays; they reflect."

"I'm back on earth," she said after a moment.

"Okay, I'll be right there."

He rolled over and kissed her, then cupped his hands over her breasts.

"I love you," she said again.

He said nothing, but nodded and smiled as if to say that he loved her or merely that he knew she did.

He thought he heard tires rolling on gravel, listened for the hum of an engine and looked for headlights. He wondered for a moment whether he was imagining it or if it was merely the sound of traffic on the highway, miles away and out of sight at the base of the mountain, that sometimes carried this far on a clear night.

"Do you hear?"

She nodded. They stared down at the road in the direction of Ritter's farm as the sound of a moving vehicle became unmistakable.

"Look!" Christine whispered. A pickup truck with its headlights and engine turned off was coasting toward them down the slight decline beyond the house. It was merely a silhouette, like that of some monstrous animal, creeping beside the orchard.

"Isn't that Ritter's truck?"

"No. There are millions of trucks like that up here."

"Let's go inside. Please! I'm scared."

"They're just spying. Lie still and they won't even see us."

The car gathered speed as it approached the house.

Staring down at it through blades of grass, Josh could see four boys lying absolutely still, like sacks of meal, in its bed. Then he saw one of them move and what appeared to be an arm extending over the edge. There was a blinding, concentrated burst of light and a violent explosion. A frame window of the farmhouse shattered and someone screamed. The re-echoing of the blast from the mountains made it seem as though dozens of distant

117

rifles had open fire upon them. Christine tried to run. Josh grabbed her and pinned her behind him. The truck was now below the house, its engine running.

"Let's get out of here!" someone shouted.

"Another one!"

"One more! What are you waiting for? Give it to me!"

Another blast slammed into one of the beams supporting the porch. Then there were four more shots in quick succession from a second-story window. Josh heard two of them strike the truck's metal.

"Get down!" screamed one of the boys.

"Go! Go!" The truck's lights flashed as it roared down the road.

Josh and Christine ran into the house. Alice and Jerry lay on the floor in front of the sofa. Peter and Mary appeared; they had crouched in the hallway after running from their rooms. Others ran down the stairs. No one had to ask what had happened.

"Is everyone here?" They glanced around at one another, frightened and subdued; most were wearing only blankets and sheets or had hastily slid into their shirts.

"The baby!" Alice lept up and ran toward the stairs.

"He's all right," said Mike. "I checked before I came down. He didn't even wake up."

Josh stared at the pistol in Pat's hand. "You said you'd gotten rid of that."

Pat shrugged. He held it to his lips and grinned as he pretended to blow smoke from its barrel.

"Are you crazy? Suppose you'd hit somebody?"

"What are we supposed to do? Bare our breasts! You go right ahead if that's what you want to do!"

"Put it away."

"Like hell! I'm going to start toting it on my hip. This is like the goddam Wild West!" Pat faced him, surprised and troubled that no one except Alice, who had reappeared with the baby, appeared to be on his side.

Then Jerry, still sitting on the floor, muttered that he thought he had been shot. Blood had begun trickling through his fingers where he held his arm. Maureen knelt and took his hand away. A grain of buckshot had grazed his bicep; a piece of flesh dangled like a shred of torn red fabric. Cyndee gasped.

"It's all right," Jerry said. "It's just a flesh wound."

"Shut up, will you?" Maureen told him. "You sound like Gary Cooper."

Jerry maintained his shell-shocked grin. "Anyway, it doesn't hurt that much. It's numb."

"You'll need stitches."

Mike said he would get dressed and take him to a doctor. He started toward his room.

"You can't go into town!" Maureen exclaimed.

"They won't hang around," Josh told her. "They'll be home in bed, thinking we've called the police. I'll go with him."

"Are you going to call them?" asked Christine.

"What's the point?"

"It wouldn't hurt."

"We don't want them up here again," said Rodney. He looked to Josh for assurance that the police would not be called.

Mike hurried back down the stairs. Josh told them to keep the lights out and to have somebody keep watch.

"If anything happens, use Ritter's phone, but don't let him know unless you have to."

Chapter Thirteen

They knew where the only doctor in the area lived, having frequently passed his shingle on the outskirts of town since they had begun driving to Simpsonville for supplies. It was a small, white frame building set very near the road, one of the few around that had obviously never been a farmhouse. Flower boxes, a lattice-worked front porch and lace curtains in the windows evidenced that its inhabitants were elderly.

Josh asked Mike and Jerry to wait in the car. He rang the bell; when no one answered he knocked upon the screen door. The hall light flashed through a small ventilation window above the door. He saw a pair of dry, frail shins beneath the hem of a bathrobe on the stairs.

"Who is it?"

"Someone's been shot."

"Who?"

"You don't know us. We live on the farm on the mountain. Ritter's place."

There was a long silence. "I know who you are."

Josh watched the old man descend past the window as he walked carefully down the stairs. No longer impatient at having his sleep interrupted he wore an expression of deep concern. He was a small man. Long white hair probably meant for a cowlick was now mussed on either side of his large, bald head; this, as well as a pair of disproportionately broad and shriveled ears, reminded Josh of his own grandfather who had died while he was at war. He hesitated again at the foot of the stairs.

"It's not a bad wound, but he'll need stitches," Josh spoke only so that the man could hear his voice, that it might relieve his fears.

"Who is it?" It was a woman's voice.

"Kids from the commune. Somebody's been shot."

"Shot! How?"

"I don't know! How do I know? They probably shot one another!"

"Someone shot at the house," Josh explained through the door.

"Someone shot at the house," the old man shouted. His wife hurried halfway down the stairs as he started to open the door.

"Don't let them in! How do you know anybody's been shot?"

"How do I know anything! At this hour how do I know anything!"

"Don't let them in," she ordered again, this time trying to threaten him with her tone of voice.

The door was pushed shut and locked again. There was another pause.

"How bad is he bleeding?"

"Not bad, but the bleeding won't stop."

"I can't treat a bullet wound. Go to the hospital in Simpsonville."

121

"It's not a bullet wound. Some buckshot passed through his arm. He only needs stitches."

"Go to the hospital!" the old woman said harshly. "Don't open that door!" she told her husband.

"They'll take care of it," the old man added.

Josh hesitated for a moment, reflecting as he stared at the floor of the porch.

"Thanks! Thanks a lot!" He hurried toward the car.

"They'll take care of it," the man said again, louder and yet more gently, as though ashamed of what he had done.

Jerry leaned out the window. "He turned you away? Why?"

"I don't know! His wife thinks we rape old women. I don't know. We'll go to the hospital."

Jerry bowed and shook his head. "No hospital."

"Why?"

"I don't trust them, that's all. I've got this thing about hospitals. Listen," he said, "forget it. It doesn't matter. It's not that bad."

A moment later Josh was knocking at the door again. The old man had been lingering behind it.

"I told you to go to the hospital."

"He won't *go* to the hospital."

"Why not?"

"He doesn't like them! He's afraid of them! I don't know!" Josh pleaded. "Would you please let him in? The rest of us will wait outside."

"Afraid! That's a lot of nonsense!"

Perhaps because he was now confronted with a type of irrationality he was used to dealing with in the natives, or simply because he was hoarse from shouting, the old man threw the door open.

"Bring him in. Only you and him. No others."

The old man eyed them closely as they entered the

house but seemed no longer to be afraid. His wife remained at a safe distance on the stairs until they had crossed through the living room and den to a smaller room that he used as an office, then she followed them. Her wrinkled nose, the lines around her eyes and upon her flaccid, hollow cheeks contributed to a seemingly frozen expression of repugnance. She wore a faded black bathrobe and clutched its collar as though afraid she might expose her withered breasts. She sat stiffly in an antique oak chair outside the office, staring but offering no assistance as her husband ministered to Jerry's arm until, suddenly, the old man frowned at her and shut the door in her face.

"It looks to me like you got a bad snag on a piece of barbed wire," he said as he applied something to stop the bleeding.

"He was shot," Josh said again.

"That's what you said. But it looks more like barbed wire to me."

Jerry grimaced as he was given a shot to deaden his arm, then he grinned sarcastically.

"That's it. I was sitting in the house minding my own business when this barbed wire fence came through the window. I ducked but it caught me before making its getaway out the back door."

"If you're going to sass me you can get out of here now."

"Wow!" muttered Jerry, ignoring his warning, his mind absorbed in the possibility of a phantom barbed wire fence.

"Shut up," Josh told him. "Just let him finish." He paced back and forth in the small room, averting his eyes from Jerry's arm as the doctor began to stitch it.

"The reason I think it's barbed wire is because if it's a buckshot wound I'll have to report it to the police."

"So what?" Jerry asked.

"There would probably be publicity and none of it would do you any good. Whether you know it or not, you don't need any more publicity." He shot several short glances at Josh as he ran the needle through Jerry's skin.

Josh frowned. "Are we supposed to believe that you're worried about us?"

"I don't care what you believe. I'm just stating a fact." He worked mechanically as he spoke, as if he were merely darning a hole in a sock. "Not too long ago a black minister moved up not too far from here. At least he called himself a minister. Some kids shot up his house. A few liberal newspapers got hold of it, and there was a stink raised that nobody could believe. Nobody left the fellow alone after that. He finally had to leave.

"Anyway," he added, "I am worried. I'm worried that somebody's going to get killed, not just shot, if you're around here much longer."

"What have we done to you?"

"Nothing. Not a thing. And I don't personally give a damn what you do up there as long as you don't move into my back yard. But I don't happen to be in the majority. I don't have to tell you that. Why'd you pick this place, anyway?"

"I wanted to live here when I was a boy."

"I'd think you'd have better sense than to try to start a place like that up here."

"It's all the same."

"Maybe. But some places are more the same than others. You know what people are like up here. They live and breath the word 'America.' How likely are they to let people live here who'd like to turn everything upside down?"

"What have we done? We haven't done anything!"

"Then you go pulling stunts like you did on the Fourth. Do you know what the Fourth of July means to them?"

"We didn't all do that."

"It doesn't matter whether you *all* did it or not. You're the rest of them and the rest of them are you. Besides, you don't have to *do* anything. Just living the way you do is enough. It's a mockery of everything these people stand for, and just being there you're a threat to them. They see this country going to hell and people like you trying to take advantage of the freedom they fought for; how likely are they just to sit back and watch?"

"Tich! Tich! To arms!" said Jerry. "We certainly don't want anyone taking advantage of freedom!" His bitterness and sarcasm were unlike him and reminded Josh increasingly of Pat.

The doctor's wife stamped her foot upon the floor to admonish him for wasting time with words. The old man frowned in her direction through the door. "You can get up now," he told Jerry. "I'm finished." He began washing his hands in a small aluminum sink.

"Where would you suggest we go?" Jerry asked.

"I don't know. But if I were to live outside of a society, I think I'd do just that instead of trying to settle down in its belly. A lot of people would like to send you to hell, but I don't feel that way. I just think there must be a better place than here."

"I sit here thinking the same thing," Jerry answered laconically, "but I just can't seem to come up with any place else. You think maybe, if we asked, the government would give us a reservation somewhere, maybe a little chunk of the Mojave Desert?"

The old man ignored him. He seemed to have been

relaxed by the performance of his work. He glanced up at Josh as he dried his hands beneath a small machine that emitted hot air.

"I've got to know whether this was from a shotgun or a piece of barbed wire."

"That's up to you," Josh said to Jerry.

"Why don't you tell everyone I took a bite out of myself while I was on a bad trip? That's what they'd like to hear."

"Barbed wire or buckshot?" the doctor asked again.

"Groovy. Barbed wire it is. What do we owe you?"

"Nothing."

"Nothing?" his wife muttered through the door.

"That's too much like a bribe. What do we owe you?"

"Five dollars."

Jerry borrowed the money from Josh to pay him.

The doctor led them to the door. The old woman stared after them but did not rise; she was evidently waiting for them to leave before launching into a tirade. They thanked him. He merely nodded.

"If you're around here much longer, I'll see you again. I'll see you again." He shut and locked the door.

Ritter, lying near an open window, unable to sleep, had heard the shotgun blasts coming from the direction of the commune. He tried to assume that it was someone coon hunting, but the incident at Fletcher's store had left him uneasy. Remembering the faces of the two Mason boys, whom he realized he did not know at all, he could not get the thought out of his head that something had happened at the commune.

Finally, he rose and dressed, took a shotgun from a cabinet and set it beside him in the pickup truck. Driving alone, studying the road for cars or hunters who might be jacking deer, he realized that he was frightened for the first time in years.

Ritter was sitting on the porch swing with the shotgun in his lap when Josh returned. Christine was seated beside him. She had offered to keep watch because she intended to stay awake for Josh, and had been with Ritter for the last hour listening, frightened by the wheezing and coughing that she thought would tear his lungs to shreds. His boots had scuffed the porch as she had gently rocked the swing. She had tried to cajole him and draw him out of his anger, to transfer to him some of the dry humor they had managed to maintain. Ritter, however, had kept his eyes trained on the road, waiting, and even hoping that the assailants would return. Together, they had looked oddly like a pair of shy lovers, each waiting for the other to make the first move.

Christine, as she met Josh in the yard, wanted to put her arms around him or at least to touch him but sensed the coldness of his mood and did not want him to know how badly she was scared.

"Did you call the police?"

"No." Josh nodded to Ritter, surprised to see him, and wondered for a moment if something else had happened.

"Why not?" Ritter snapped.

"You could have called them, Josh. It couldn't have hurt."

"It wouldn't do any good."

"How do you know?" Ritter snarled. "You don't know!"

Josh sat on the porch rail and divided his attention between them.

"Pat and I had an apartment in the Village before we came up here. One night someone tried to break in, so we called the police. When they finally came they took one look at us and told us that if we called them again they'd stick an envelope of heroin in our pockets and arrest us for possession."

"Possession of what?" Ritter asked.

"The heroin they'd stick in our pockets!"

"They couldn't do that!" Christine exclaimed.

Josh grinned. "Why not? They could have done it the other night if they'd thought about it. They probably just haven't caught onto that trick up here."

Ritter pondered for a moment what Josh had said. Then he sniffed, rubbed his nose and glared up at him.

"So, what are you going to do about it?"

Josh shrugged.

"Nothing?"

"What are we supposed to do?"

"Fight them! Get yourselves ready for the next time they come back."

"Who'd win if we started fighting them? Don't you see how easy it would be for them to get rid of us?"

"You'd win! Nobody'd win!" Ritter waved the shotgun angrily. "I'm not talking about a war. I'm talking about letting them know that you're ready to blow their heads off if they come up here again. You got any guns around here?"

"No. There's a pistol, but there won't be after tonight."

"A pistol! You might as well unzip your fly and aim that at them for all the good it would do!" He smiled then grimaced with embarrassment as he remembered Christine was there.

"Take this!" He held the shotgun out to Josh. Josh shook his head and refused it.

"I'd leave before I'd use one of those again."

"They could kill you! All of you! And there's no way you could stop them."

"They're not going to kill us. They're just trying to scare us."

"Scare you!" Ritter barked. "What was the bandage on that boy's arm?"

Josh said nothing, afraid that the old man's strength would not sustain his anger, that he would collapse where he sat on the swing. He closed his eyes and rubbed them, then glanced at Christine who, tired and drawn, was waiting for him near the door.

"Go ahead," he said quietly. "I'll be up in a few minutes." She hesitated, then went inside.

Ritter coughed then spat contemptuously over the porch rail. He frowned up at Josh, then nodded toward the shotgun. Whatever restraint he had exercised in front of Christine was suddenly gone.

"You won't take it?"

"No."

"Then you're a fool."

Josh winced. Realizing for the first time the depth of his attachment to the old man, he stood for several moments leaning against a porch beam and staring at the floor.

"I can't explain, but if I took it I wouldn't have anything left. It would be the end of everything. It wouldn't matter if the commune lasted."

Ritter, staring past him toward the road, pretended that he was not listening. He, too, seemed to have been hurt by his own words. Josh offered to drive him home.

"I'm staying here."

"You don't need to."

"I don't! Not if you'll take this. But I'm not leaving you here without it."

"Then come inside and sleep."

Ritter shook his head. Josh sat beside him, setting the swing in motion involuntarily. Listening to Ritter's wheezing, he remembered again the old papa-san he had seen tortured by Vietnamese near a burning hootch. Josh, lying in a litter and awaiting medical evacuation, had watched while they nearly suffocated the old man by holding a wet cloth to his mouth and nose. When he lost consciousness, they poured water over his face. Staring and blinking at the clouds, he seemed out of reach of the men who tortured him, with all his terror concentrated in and relinquished to the constant rhythm of his breath.

When Josh had screamed for them to stop, they had thought him delirious, as if they could not conceive that a white man could consider their actions wrong. They had dipped the cloth in water and held it over the old man's face again, grinning involuntarily as they often did when torturing someone. This time, when he no longer writhed, they had removed the cloth, seen that his eyes were open and gotten up to leave him for dead. Then someone noticed that his heart was beating and realized they had been tricked. The old man had merely been lying there staring through them taking small, undetectable breaths, utterly self-possessed.

At dawn Josh was awakened by Ritter's truck pulling away from the house. The musty blanket Ritter had found and laid over him was damp with dew; he spread it to dry on the porch rail and watched until the truck was out of sight. Then he went inside, undressed and lay in bed beside Christine, who had not slept.

Chapter Fourteen

They awoke late that morning and ate breakfast together. Seated around the long, low plank table that Peter had constructed, they discussed steps they could begin taking to defend themselves. Pat, brooding, left as soon as he saw that there was overwhelming opposition to his pistol or weapons of any sort. Alice was the only other militant; feeling herself a newcomer she merely stated her sympathy with Pat and did not argue. Her ruddy biceps flexed impressively as she raised Horace to her shoulders and began to feed him. Horace, his chin on her head, grabbed for the spoon each time it neared him. Hot cereal and orange juice dripped upon Alice's hair, but she ignored it, smiling handsomely.

Mike asked if she would like him to drive her to the city where she and the baby could wait until things grew calmer. She said no, that she hoped numberless, nonexistent Horace would someday lead the revolution and that life on the commune, as it appeared to be becoming, would provide him with invaluable preparation. Horace grabbed the spoon from her hand and began beating her forehead. He grinned, nodding his fat, bald head as if in appreciation of their laughter.

"Being born without a number is the next best thing to Immaculate Conception," Jerry explained. "He's bound to be a leader in something."

Unable to give the crisis the serious attention it deserved, they whimsically imagined an escalating cold war with the natives. They pictured a barbed wire encampment that would include the perimeter of Ritter's orchards, an apple grenade factory and machine guns that sprayed apple seeds, and rockets that would hurl red ripe apple satellites into orbit. They imagined a mammoth American apple pie baked by Cyndee and containing the Apple Bomb; they would wheel it like a Trojan horse to the edge of the village where it would explode once the population had been wooed by its fragrant odor. The only real decision they arrived at regarding their own safety was that someone would have to stay up each night and keep watch.

The mailman drove by and deliberately wrenched their box as he left a note and a letter. The note stated that the box was in disrepair and that he would leave no more mail until it met government standards. The letter was for Mike from a friend who lived on a commune in Colorado. After months of harrassment the commune had been closed by health authorities when one of its members was hospitalized with hepatitis. Five diehards were now interested in coming to Vermont and wondered whether they would be welcome. Cyndee noted that the harvest was unlikely to produce enough food for the eleven of them, much less half again that number, but they all quickly agreed that Mike should write and invite them to come.

During his morning walk Josh had decided that at least a small part of the crop was ready for harvest. Most of the group went into the field after breakfast and began pacing the long rows, picking and uprooting vegetables that had matured. Josh and Christine set off in the Nash on a tour of junk shops outside the radius of town, searching for the hundreds of jars they would need for canning.

They passed a police car about ten miles outside of town. Paxton stared, then swung around in the road to follow them, tailgating for about two miles but giving no indication that he wanted them to stop.

"What's he trying to do?" Christine asked.

"We haven't done anything. He's just playing Joe Friday."

"He's doing a good job!" Christine laughed nervously and leaned back in the seat with her hands in the pockets of her jeans. "I think he was waiting for us."

"Why doesn't he *pass?*" she said finally.

Josh signaled and pulled to the side of the road. Paxton pulled off behind them, parked and strode toward them deliberately with notebook in hand.

"Get out."

"What have we done?"

"Get out! Both of you!" He leaned over and eyed Christine through the open door. "Slide out on this side and leave the door open. Lean with your hands against the roof."

Paxton ran his hands down Josh's chest, past his

pockets, and even felt in his socks for hidden razor blades and packets of dope. He made Josh empty his wallet, then started to frisk Christine.

"Don't touch her," Josh said quietly. "You don't need to do this."

Paxton's eyes widened. He shoved Josh against the door.

"Turning around like that's a good way to get shot! How do I know you're not trying to pull a gun?"

"Because you just searched me!"

"It's all right," Christine whispered.

"I wouldn't touch you, either of you, if I didn't have to! I wouldn't look at you!"

Paxton felt the pockets of Christine's shirt and jeans, then examined her socks with extra care as if he had learned somewhere that this was where addicts often hid their works. He studied Josh's license and registration then examined the inside of the car without putting his head through the door.

"Your car?"

"Yes."

"You sure?"

"Yes!"

"This your name?" he waved Josh's license.

"Yes."

"You sure?"

"Yes!!"

He wrote Josh's name on the pad, gripping the pen tightly with his large, dark hand. Christine noticed the apparent difficulty with which he wrote and, for a moment, felt sorry for him. Two cars passed slowly, their occupants grinning and nodding at Paxton, who nodded in return. He ordered Christine to give him some

134

document with her name on it.

"I don't have anything with me."

"You don't have a wallet or a purse?" He seemed positive that she was lying.

Christine shook her head.

"I could arrest you for vagrancy."

"I didn't know that," she answered simply.

He handed her the pad and had her write her name. When she had finished he placed a large question mark beside it. An old, flower-painted ambulance with New York plates passed. The youths inside it stared knowingly upon Josh's situation and gave the sign of peace. Josh returned it. Paxton smirked and began firing his questions even more quickly.

"Where are you going?"

"To buy jars."

"What for?"

"Canning."

"Canning what?"

"Vegetables!"

Abruptly, Paxton returned Josh's license, strode back to his car and raced off, tires squealing, after the ambulance.

"Our friend the policeman," Christine nervously tried to smile. "I guess he's got a full-time job."

"Maybe someday we'll outnumber them."

"We'll make them go naked in the summer so they'll be embarrassed to get out of their cars."

"Or let Pat put them up against the wall."

She looked at him carefully. "Do you mean that?"

"No." He forced a smile, but his lips quivered with anger.

Josh thought of Pat's pistol, then imagined Pat and

himself robbing a bank, Pat demanding all the money the teller had while Josh trained a machine gun on Paxton, the bank guard. He imagined Paxton going for his holster, then saw himself severing the man's neck with bullets, his head rolling upon the floor as the teller filled a burlap sack with green vegetables. He imagined the two of them racing out the door, then roaring away in Paxton's police car with the siren wailing.

While they were gone a bizarre demonstration was held across the road from the farm. Potter, the local Boy Scoutmaster, had obtained permission from the parents of five of the fifteen boys in his pack to hold a brief, patriotic assembly, promising that he would keep the children a safe distance from the commune and that he would have a pistol handy in his truck.

The boys, ages twelve through fourteen, sat solemnly and apprehensively in the back of the pickup as Potter drove them up the mountain. He parked; the oldest boy stood in the truck, holding an American flag that waved and snapped in the wind as the others stood at attention behind him facing the farm. Potter climbed out then led them through all three verses of the national anthem. Their frightened, shrill, pubescent voices somehow managed to blend and even sound inspiring.

The members of the commune gathered on the porch to listen. Rodney, who was stoned, leaned back on his elbows and shook his head dully.

"Wow," he muttered to no one, "it's scary. I mean it's *really* scary, you know?" He looked at Mike. "I mean someday all these red-neck kids are going to be thirty and we're going to be thirty and there's going to be one hell of a civil war."

"Maybe we ought to beat them up while we still can," Mike grinned. Peter looked at him disapprovingly until he was sure that he was kidding.

"Give them some cookies," Maureen said to Cyndee. "Maybe we can convert them."

Cyndee, looking like anyone's plump homely sister, walked down the yard holding a wooden platter covered with cookies.

"Stay away from them!" Potter barked. "Stay on your side."

The children stared at her. Some of them mimicked Potter's snarl; others were merely scared. Potter began singing "America," obviously proud of his baritone voice. The boys joined him. When they had finished, Potter guarded them until they were seated. He glared at the farm and grinned to himself before climbing back behind the wheel. The group waved to the children. One of them waved back instinctively, then drew in his arm and hunched his shoulder as he was reprimanded by the others.

That evening, just before dark, Pat walked out the front door with a duffel bag and met Josh sitting alone on the porch.

"Sin-loy."

"What do you mean?"

"I'm heading south."

"Why?" Josh asked.

Pat shrugged.

"Don't be an ass! Why? Because of that?" He nodded to the bulge in Pat's vest where he was now wearing his pistol in a holster.

"Martyrdom's not my bag. Anyway, I don't belong around here. You know that."

137

"There's nothing to belong to. This isn't a club."

"That's so much crap!" Pat answered bitterly. "Christ! Sometimes you reek with platitudes." They stood facing one another and sensed the barrier of pride that had drawn between them over the past weeks. Pat averted his eyes from Josh, staring past the road at the orchard as he spoke again.

"Okay, so there's nothing to belong to. Let's just say I'm not the kind of person who belongs on a commune. I feel as though everyone around here is always accusing me of something."

"They're not."

"I know that! That's not the point. The point is you're the way you are and I'm the way I am and, for one thing, I'm not interested in sitting up here and being a clay pigeon."

"Where are you going?" Josh asked again.

"I don't know." Again he shrugged, speaking more quietly, as though sorry for some of the things he had said. "Probably New York. I've got some things in mind. I'll let you know."

"You don't have to leave tonight."

"Yes, I do. If I stay till morning everyone will try to talk me out of leaving and I'll feel like more of a bastard. Besides, leaving at night is symbolic." He grinned then nodded and started down the yard.

"I may be back. I don't know."

"Do you want a ride to town?" Josh asked, walking with him to the road.

"No."

At the road Pat wished Josh luck and, with tongue in cheek, made the sign of peace in the direction of the house.

138

"I'll drop you a note when I know where I am."

Christine, who had paused inside the screen door when she had heard them talking, walked out onto the porch as Josh climbed back up the yard.

"Why?" she whispered.

Josh shrugged, but Christine sensed that she was, somehow, at least partly to blame.

Only the living room windows of Ritter's farmhouse were dimly lighted. The front door was open. Josh knocked gently on the screen door in order not to wake the old man if he had gone to bed early, but Ritter shouted immediately from somewhere in the darkness.

"Who is it?"

"Josh."

"Come in!"

Josh walked through the hallway to the living room where a small, flickering fire provided the only illumination. Ritter was nearly lost in the bowels of an old stuffed chair; its sagging back and bent springs were tailored to the contour of his frail body. It was pulled close to the fire, and had been since the last evening Josh and Christine had visited him. Ritter did not glance up from the fire when Josh entered the room; Josh wondered if the old man was still mad at him.

"Sit down." Ritter jerked his arm toward an empty chair beside him.

"I've come to ask you to dinner. We did some early harvesting today and we're holding sort of a feast."

"Sit down!"

Josh slid over the arm of the empty chair. He watched the firelight dancing and accenting the lines on the old man's face. Finally, drawn by Ritter's fascination with the flames, Josh looked at them, too, and was absorbed by the pulsing coals. He thought of the deer he had found in the road and the doe that had stared, overwhelmed by his headlights, and wondered what sort of monstrous animal a deer thought a car was at night.

The acrid scent of old age that hung in each room of the house, and on the fabric of every chair, was mixed with the sweet scent of burning apple logs. The firelight stirred the darkness, reflected upon the glass and seemed to eliminate the sense of time passing.

"Any more trouble?"

"No."

"There will be."

"Maybe not."

"There will be."

"We're keeping watch."

"What for? Waste of time. Watch is all you'll do. Watch yourselves get shot."

Ritter shook his head slowly and frowned at the fire. He bent forward with a cough, then settled back, expressionless, with his thin arms resting on the arms of the chair.

"Suppose I give you this place?" he asked quietly. "Suppose I give it to you. Not just the old farm, but this place and all the orchards and the land." He turned to relish Josh's expression of shock.

"Why?"

"Why not?" Ritter snapped.

"Because it's yours."

"I know it's mine! I couldn't give it to you if it wasn't mine!"

"Why would you want to do it? I don't understand."

"Because I want to! Because I know what's going to

happen to this place when I die. I'd will it to you, but if I did you'd never get it. Willing something to somebody is a sure way of seeing that they never get it. So, I'll sell it to you for a dollar. But it'll stay mine, more or less, till I die."

"I couldn't do it."

"Why?"

"I'd feel as if I were using you. I'd feel too guilty about it."

"I've been using you. Hasn't bothered me." He glanced sharply at Josh. "You ever think what will happen to you and your commune when I die. They'd have you out of here, legally, in a month. You want that?"

"No."

"Suppose I die tomorrow?"

"You won't."

"Ha! Thanks! So the day after tomorrow or next month or next year." He propped himself up in the chair, then fumbled in the pockets of his coat for a cigarette. He lit the cigarette and threw the match at the fire. It lay smoldering on the hardwood floor.

"How long do you think it will be before I have to have someone wait on me? How long before I won't have enough strength left to stop them from putting me in a home? Five years? Ten? I want to be dead by then. I'll be sure to be dead by then! How long do you expect your commune to last?"

"I don't know."

"What do you mean, you don't know? A year? Ten? Twenty? You want it to last, don't you?"

"Yes."

"Well, the only way it's going to last is if you own

this land! And that's the only way the orchards are going to last, or any of it. If you don't take it, then all of it dies when I die, which means it's more or less dead already."

"You don't even know me that well! There must be somebody else."

"Don't I? Who *do* I know? Don't I? Don't tell me who I know!" Ritter rasped, then, tired of words, settled back in his chair. "There's nobody else I'd even sell to. You want it or don't you?"

Josh imagined the commune including all of Ritter's property. He thought of Mike's friends who would arrive soon, of more youths, many more, and enough children to start a school. He imagined Ritter's remaining woods cleared and planted with apple trees. He imagined a community large enough to be observed and, perhaps, emulated by the outside world. He smiled at himself, wondering whether his motives had always been so mundane.

In every picture that came into his head there was Ritter, shuffling, cursing, spitting and observing it all with an impatient frown. He would not let himself imagine the commune without the old man.

"Yes. I want it."

Ritter nodded to himself and smiled briefly. He took several long breaths and nodded, again, at the fire.

"I'll have the papers made out tomorrow."

"Will you come to dinner? They're waiting for us."

"No."

"Why not?"

"Too much fuss!"

"I won't tell them tonight if you don't want me to."

"Too much fuss. Besides, you don't eat meat, do you?"

"No."

"Then it'd be a waste of time. I'd just have to eat again. Stop down for breakfast, you and the girl." Ritter always referred to Christine as "the girl." He had forgotten her name as soon as Josh told him and never asked it again.

Josh stood and hovered near the fire. Its dry warmth appeared to have made Ritter tired; he rubbed his wrinkled forehead with the palm of his hand.

"Thanks."

"Don't!" Ritter snapped. "You still don't want one of those?" He nodded toward the rifle case in the corner.

Josh shook his head. He said good night. The old man neither stood nor turned to watch as Josh left.

The information Paxton had received on a teletype that afternoon had not proved entirely disappointing; it told him that Josh had been discharged as mentally unfit for the army. Potter learned of this an hour later, and by evening nearly everyone who had attended the meeting received some exaggerated "proof" that the boy whom they had discussed that night was crazy. Even those who had refused to take Potter seriously before were now worried.

Chapter Fifteen

Mike, lying on his elbow near the top of the roof, was singing an aria in Italian complete with operatic inflections. He waved and began climbing down the ladder when he saw Josh coming up the road.

"Oh solo mio!" he called. "What took you so long? Where's Ritter."

"He wouldn't come."

"Why?"

Josh said simply that Ritter was tired.

Lanterns were blown out and candles were lighted in the dining room. Mary had made a linen cape for Jerry; it was printed with horns of plenty especially for the occasion. He threw it gallantly over his shoulders, tied its nylon cord, then stood at the head of the table and raised his arms inside it, uttering a pompous and long-winded incantation of thanks to the spirit of vegetation over a wooden platter piled with pale golden ears of young corn.

144

A cauldron of vegetarian stew was carried from the kitchen. They sat on the table and in one another's laps on the chairs eating, symbolically, from the same bowl. Josh remained aloof beside Christine. He felt guilty that Ritter had, in effect, given him his life, and decided to wait until the morning to tell them, not wanting the announcement to play a part in the celebration. He felt guilty, too, for keeping this secret from them, but told himself that he needed time to think.

They talked about the possibility of buying a second-hand cow, as Jerry called it, with the little money they might save now that they no longer needed to buy most of their food. Ritter, they knew, intended to pay them extra, by the bushel, for the apples they would begin picking in a month. Maureen had found a tourist shop outside of Simpsonville that had agreed to sell her pots for a commission. They talked, also, about the possibility of inviting friends up to stay now that they could afford to feed them. Cyndee mentioned the idea of getting a farm dog. There was very little reference to Pat. No one claimed to know why he had left. Yet in a way they all did, and all of them felt partly to blame.

It was nearly midnight when Peter, who had taken a walk, as he often did by himself, turned back up the road toward the farm. He heard the car before its headlights swept around a curve and encompassed him. It slowed and its engine revved behind him as he moved further to the side of the road. He did not need to turn to see who it was, recognized its broken muffler and knew it was the rusty, dented, two-tone Chevy that had passed the farm so many times during the last few months. He slid his hands into his pockets and stared directly ahead as the car nudged up beside him.

There were five boys in it. Henry was driving. His brother sat beside him.

"You're real pretty," Henry said.

"*Real* pretty," Cal added. The boys in the back seat laughed.

Peter continued to ignore them. Beads of sweat gathered on his forehead but he did not reach to wipe them. Henry kept revving the engine, letting Peter walk ahead into the light then popping the clutch and roaring up beside him. Peter's knees began to weaken. He tried to concentrate his strength in them, to keep them from giving way, and kept walking.

"I mean you're real pretty," Henry whined again. "Real pretty."

"Real pretty."

"I mean I'd say he's beautiful. Wouldn't you?"

"I'd say so."

One of the boys in the back seat giggled. Another threw a beer bottle out the window, barely missing Peter's head.

"I mean look at that hair. And those beads. I feel like picking you a flower. I think I'd like to walk with you. Wouldn't you?" Cal nodded.

Peter thought of trying to outrun them through the orchard. He thought of turning and facing them. Instead, he continued walking, closing his eyes briefly to clear the blood from his head and fighting his urge to walk faster.

The two boys walked on either side of him in the headlights. The other three stood beside the parked car, watching.

"You're so pretty I'd like to hold your hand. Say! Maybe you'd like to blow me!" The other boys laughed.

Henry grabbed Peter's arm. Peter stopped and faced him. Suddenly, Henry pushed him, and he tumbled over Cal, who had crouched behind him.

"Get up!"

"I'm not going to fight you," Peter said quietly.

"You will or I'll kick your brains out!"

Peter stood slowly and put his hands back into his pockets to make sure that he would not use them. He closed his eyes a split second before Henry's fist struck him, heard the bridge of his nose crack and saw a white, blinding light as he staggered backward. His mind played tricks. He thought that the blood on his face was sweat or water; then he tasted it and remembered what was happening. Henry kneed him in the groin. He lay curled and writhing on his side, wanting to beg them or at least to moan, but not letting himself make a sound.

"Get up! Hit me!'" Henry screamed.

Peter rose to his knees and was blinded by the headlights. Then stood, nearly doubled over.

"I'm not going to fight." He thought of putting his hands in his pockets again, then realized he could no longer fight even if he tried. He wondered why the boy cared if he defended himself, why he seemed to want Peter to hit him.

"You'll fight or I'll kill you!"

"No," he whispered. Henry hit him again. He fell and no longer tried to stand.

"Let's go! He won't fight!" shouted one of the boys by the car.

Henry and Cal started toward them. Then Cal ran back, took the beads from around Peter's neck and kicked him in the spine. He trotted toward the car, holding out the beads and grinning to his friends. Henry squealed the tires in reverse until he found a place to turn around.

"He's not so pretty anymore," said Cal. They laughed, but all of them were scared by the crumpled shadow they saw behind them as the car sped off.

Peter did not move until they were gone. Then he sat up, unbuttoned his shirt and folded it in his hands. He wiped his face with the shirt, careful not to touch his nose. He remembered a time when he was six years old, how two boys he thought were his best friends had ganged up on him after he had beaten them individually in playful wrestling matches. He remembered how the three of them had been sitting together, their legs dangling from the edge of a porch; how it had grown quiet and how the two boys had suddenly pulled him to the ground. He remembered how they had hit him, and how his own fist had shot out involuntarily and shattered the nose of one of the boys. He remembered how he had burst into tears at the sight of the blood and how he had run home and hidden in a cabin behind the garage; how he had sat in the cabin and cried for himself, not because he was hurt—he was hardly bruised—but for the memory of his own fist striking the other boy and, most of all, because he didn't understand.

Peter sat with the blood-stained shirt in his hand, drops of blood spattering on his chest and pants, laughed at himself and shook his head because he was crying.

He walked up the yard to the farmhouse. His face was smeared with blood; it had dried and caked in rivulets beneath his nose and down his neck. He was introverted, as always, studying the ground as he walked. Perhaps he would have walked directly to the kitchen pump, washed himself and said nothing of what had happened had it been possible to do so. However, Cyndee, who was the first to see him, screamed. Moments later he was surrounded, everyone asking what had happened.

Peter intermittently grinned and made faces as Mary, crying, wiped the blood from his face with a wet cloth. Christine stood near Josh. He stared, expressionless, and said nothing.

Upstairs, the baby began to wail. Jerry brought him down, then stood bouncing him in his arms.

Peter seemed proud, in his shy way, that he had not fought them. He said that he had always called himself a pacifist but had never known whether he would be able to turn the other cheek if attacked. Jerry told him that he *should* have turned the other cheek, that if he had he might have been left with a nose. Peter bowed his head and smiled. Then he shook his head and glanced up at the others.

"Man, they hate us. I mean they really do."

"What did they look like?" Josh asked.

"They were just kids."

"I know that!" Josh said angrily. "What did they look like?"

"Your friends, I think."

Josh walked onto the porch, then toward the road. Christine watched him through the screen door, then followed him as he went into the orchard. She found him near the base of it, out of sight of the house, and sat beside him. She put her head on his shoulder and her arms around him but he did not move.

"I'm scared."

He nodded.

"I'm scared of you, too. I don't want to be but I can't help it."

"Why?"

"You're letting this change you. You're so far away that I wonder if you're there."

"I'm here."

"What are you thinking?"

"About Pat."

"That wouldn't do any good. You've said so yourself."

"What will?"

"They can't keep doing this forever."

"Why not?"

"They can't! If Peter had fought them, if he'd beaten them, they'd come after him again. They won't now that they know he won't fight them."

"You think they won't *tyrannize* him every time they see him?"

"If you fight them you're just like they are; they've won. That's what you looked like this morning when the cop pushed you; you looked just like him. I thought you could kill him."

"I could."

"Why?" she pleaded. "Because he touched me?"

Josh frowned at her, then sat silently. He did not hold her when he saw that she was crying; instead, he began, quietly, to tell her about the old man he had seen tortured.

"But he won, didn't he?" she asked. "Isn't that the point?"

"When they saw his heart beating they thought he'd

been trying to fool them. One of them got mad and shot him in the head. They dumped him down a well to pollute the water."

"Don't!" she sobbed.

"I killed two people over there before I stopped to think what I was doing. So is it that I've changed or that I haven't changed? Who should I have killed, them or that cop? Or those boys?"

"Please!"

He looked at her and realized that he had been trying to hurt her because she did not know, or have to know, about any of those things.

"I'm sorry."

She had closed her eyes, like a child trying to shut herself off from something unbearable. He stood in the darkness and picked a large, green apple. He set it in her lap, then knelt beside her and told her what had happened at Ritter's.

"Not just the old farm" he explained. "Everything. The orchards and everything."

"You mean he's going to will it to you?"

"He's *giving* it to me. In the next few days."

She stared at him in amazement. "Why?"

"He's afraid of what will happen to it when he dies."

"Josh, that's fabulous!" She threw her arms around him. "Are you sure he wasn't just in one of his moods?"

"He meant it. He'd been thinking about it for a long time."

"That means it's going to last! It will have to now, won't it?"

He nodded. "We might even be able eventually to make enough money to build some more houses."

"And people will stay. I'm always afraid they're going

to leave sooner or later. It's hard to imagine us all still here when we're middle-aged."

"I'd rather not," he laughed.

"There'd be room for more—Jerry's friends."

"More than that. We might have enough nonexistent kids to start a school. And it could mean something. You know?"

She lay her head on his shoulder and he rocked her back and forth.

"You've never talked about any of those things," she whispered.

"The war?"

"Yes."

"Did you want me to?"

"No." She shook her head. "I don't think so. No."

They walked back up to the farmhouse. Peter and Mary were seated on the porch swing, rocking it. The squeaking of its rusty chains reminded Christine of Ritter's wheezing.

"I'll keep watch," Josh said.

"That's all right," Peter answered. "My back hurts. I can't sleep anyway."

"You want to go to a doctor?"

Peter shook his head.

"You'll have to," Mary told him. "Your nose is all the way around on the side of your head."

Peter grinned. "Maureen can fix it. It's like working with clay."

They said good night.

Chapter Sixteen

Peter and Mary, searching for constellations in order to stay awake, heard nothing when the back door was opened nor when a five-gallon bucket of kerosene was poured slowly across the kitchen floor. When a burning rag was tossed on the floor, it was less like an explosion than a violent gust of wind—as if a huge trailer truck had somehow passed directly behind them. The front porch was flooded with light. By the time Peter reached the door, the kitchen and most of the dining room were already engulfed in flames. For a second both of them stood pertrified, then Peter ran into the house screaming and shielding his face from the heat. Mary yelled to him as he disappeared up the stairs, then ran inside and began beating on all the bedroom doors she could reach.

As Christine and Josh slid frantically into their jeans, Peter threw open their door.

"There's no time!" he pleaded.

They ran out of the room. Jerry and Alice, with the baby, were huddled at the top of the stairs rubbing their eyes from the black smoke that poured up the stairwell. Staring down it, Josh could see nothing but smoke and flames that, fed by fresh paint, had begun sliding like jelly up the walls.

Peter yelled to them. They followed him down the hallway into Alice's and Jerry's front bedroom. Smoke poured into the room after them. Peter held the window open until they had all climbed onto the porch roof, tossed out a handful of clothing that lay on a chair, then scrambled after them.

"Here!" Mike shouted. He raised a ladder against the roof. They climbed down, Alice in one of Jerry's long shirts and Jerry in his cape, holding the baby.

"Ritter's!" Josh yelled to Mike. "Call the fire department." Mike ran down the yard toward the hearse.

"Is everybody here?"

"Everybody except Cyndee," Maureen answered. She nodded toward a bedroom window from which clothing and luggage were being thrown.

"Water!" Josh screamed. "Get the buckets!"

Rodney ran from behind the house where the fire buckets had been stacked. "There aren't any buckets! They're gone!"

Josh ran to look for himself where they had been by the kitchen door. Then, dazed, he looked up at the house. The kitchen was lost in flames that swirled and swelled with air sucked through the open windows and door. He had an urge to run through the door and into the flames. He looked at the fire and saw himself, his clothing burning, and imagined the breath of fire in his lungs.

"Buckets wouldn't help," Rodney said. "We'd never stop it."

Josh looked at him, then at the others who had followed him. Christine took his arm. They knew, all of them, how the fire had started. The putrid scent of kerosene still hung in the air.

"I didn't hear them," Peter moaned, thinking Josh's blank stare an accusation.

Josh said nothing. He drew his arm away from Christine, slid his hands into the pockets of his jeans and walked away from the house. He sat at the edge of the field, with his bare arms wrapped around his knees, and watched the fire. In their haste they had left most of the windows and doors open. The flames, sucked up the stairwell like smoke up a chimney, began lighting the second story windows. Smoke poured out the windows and through cracks in the eaves that he had not known were there.

He looked at the others nearer the house, dazed and wandering in a small circle, like sheep. He watched Christine, bare-breasted and silhouetted against the firelight, walk toward him with two shirts dangling from her hand. For a moment, he hated her simply because she was closest to him. She stood above him, her lips pressed firmly together and her eyes glazed.

"Let's go for a walk," she whispered. He shook his head and stared past her. The roar of the fire grew continually louder. The others began withdrawing as the heat grew more intense.

"Josh! Please! Don't look at it!" She knelt beside him, too afraid of him to touch him.

"Please," she begged.

He watched Cyndee, a large black ball, leap out her

window. He saw Peter, who had climbed in Mike's window to save what he could, leap out of the side of the house. He watched the others, shadows, scavenging the ground for clothes.

"Please!"

He glanced at her, then pulled her down beside him. She buried her head in his lap, sobbing.

Fletcher was head of the volunteer fire department. For this reason, and because he would have been so opposed as to try to prevent it, he had not been told that the farm was going to be burned. Moments after the phone rang, he pressed a button that set off an alarm outside a new, concrete building that housed two trucks belonging to the town. By the time he reached the fire station, every house in town was lighted. Potter and Mason, two other volunteers, were waiting for him.

"Slow down!" Potter exclaimed. "Where's the fire?"

Potter grinned, but Mason, frightened and subdued, merely stared at the ground.

When Mike returned with Ritter the frame of the house still stood, containing what appeared to be one immense ball of flame that cast a twilight illumination over the orchards. Ritter cocked his head, staring viciously up at the house. Mike lept out and ran around to open his door.

"Get away!" Ritter snapped.

He opened the door himself, climbed out of the hearse slowly and mechanically, then shuffled up the yard, his frail arms dangling as limp as rope at his sides. The others watched silently from where they sat near the field as Ritter stopped about thirty feet away from the house, directly in front of it. Leaning toward the fire, with his head bowed to protect his face from the heat, he appeared grotesquely hunchbacked and in prayer. His bald head glowed. His shoulders rose and fell with his breath. He stared at the fire as though hypnotized or deeply in thought, with his small hands protected from the heat inside the pockets of his old coat.

There was a thunderous crash as part of the ceiling collapsed, spewing sparks and embers in a cloud of smoke out the porch window. With this the fire seemed to hesitate, then momentarily redoubled in its intensity. Ritter, jarred out of his trance, contorted his face as the heat pressed against it and began nodding as though the cackling and hissing of burning timbers were voices speaking to him.

He turned as Josh moved into his vision. They faced and stared at one another and understood one another without words. It was as though, for the first time, their visions of life were utterly the same. Without a sound, or the slightest change in their expressions, Ritter asked Josh a question, and Josh answered. Finally, Ritter sucked his lips into his gums, spat at the ground and spoke.

"You know who did it?"

"No."

"I could guess. But it wouldn't do any good."

"No."

"Doesn't matter. It was built lousy. Bad location; the ground here shifts around every spring. Doubt that we could have done much with the foundation.

"You can move in with me in the morning. Make enough from picking apples to buy yourself some new clothes."

"No."

"No what? The place is yours. Or it will be within a few days."

"I can't take it. Not now."

"You'll take it," Ritter answered firmly. "The deed will be made out in the morning."

"What do you want them to do, burn that too?" Josh pleaded. "I can't take it! Can't you see?"

Ritter, breathing asthmatically and clutching the lapel of his coat, refused to hear Josh or look at him. He stared at the fire.

"I'll make out the deed in the morning."

"I won't sign it! You want to save this place, don't you? Isn't that why you were giving it to me?" Ritter didn't answer. "You call this saving it? You want to see the whole thing burned down around you?"

"They won't burn my place."

"Wouldn't they? Why not? Did you think they'd do this?"

Again, Ritter ignored him. His face was tired and drawn. For the first time he appeared even older than he was. There was another loud crash and roar of flames as a portion of the roof collapsed.

"Giving up," he finally muttered.

"They're scared! I couldn't keep them here even if I thought it was right."

"You?"

"I want to stay. Maybe Christine. There's no place else. They might leave the two of us alone."

Ritter's eyes came back to life. "Stay at my place. It'll be yours."

"I can't take it. Let's not talk about it anymore. Your old cabin. Would that be all right?"

Ritter nodded. He studied Josh closely. "You going to let them come in and burn it?"

"They won't come near it."

"Good! Good."

The fire trucks arrived, followed by a seemingly endless procession of volunteers and sight-seeing natives. Ritter watched as Fletcher and several others officiously turned knobs and unwound hoses. He watched as Potter and Mason, in black slickers and helmets, began dragging one of the hoses up the hill. Then he stepped in their path.

"Needn't bother."

"What do you mean?" Potter asked impatiently.

"Can't save it. Waste of good water."

"Did everyone get out?" Mason asked. Ritter glared at him, then nodded.

Bill Ferguson, clambering up the hill behind them, had overheard. "We need the practice," he said. "This is the first big fire we've had in two years."

"Fancy that!"

Potter's face grew firm. "There's a law against letting a fire rage out of control like this. You'd better let us by."

"You're trespassing!" Ritter snapped. "Get off my land! Hold it!" he shouted to Fletcher who, with two other men, had started up the hill with another hose.

"Get back in the road! Let it burn! Burn!"

A patrol car sped up the mountain, its siren wailing. Paxton and another trooper trotted up the yard, their bellies bouncing.

"What are you waiting for?" Paxton asked, when he realized that nothing was being done.

"He won't let us put it out!" Ferguson told him.

Paxton turned to Ritter. "Is that right?"

"It is."

"Tell him there's a law against it!" Potter exclaimed. "This thing could spread."

"There is. You'd better get out of the way."

"Get off my property," Ritter said quietly. "Or arrest me if you want to. But you'll have to drag me away, and if you do that some of my bones are liable to break." He grinned maliciously and gathered his breath. "Old bones like mine don't heal. More than likely it would kill me. It would look kind of bad to burn down a man's house and kill him too."

Paxton looked down at him and ran his tongue across his lips. He looked at Potter and the other volunteers, who were wiping sweat from their faces and fidgeting impatiently inside their shimmering, fire-lit slickers.

"Let it burn," he told them. "You can't save it. Spray around it if it starts to spread."

"Now get off my property!" Ritter gesticulated as though shooing flies, then turned to Paxton. "All of you!"

Slowly and angrily they returned to the road. When they dropped their hoses and turned to stare at him, he smiled. Another section of roof collapsed, but Ritter did not glance back at it. Instead, he looked up and down the road at the men, women and children, at the firelight flickering on their faces as they stared back at him. Then he lowered himself awkwardly to the ground and sat between them and the house. Out of the corner of his eye he saw a carload of youths laughing and talking, sipping beer when they thought no one was watching. Behind them, the leaves and branches of the apple trees were alive with the shifting light.

Josh and Christine sat near the pond, out of sight of the crowd. Its smooth surface reflected the fire so that it seemed that the water itself was aflame except where their shadows slithered across it.

"Will you stay?" he asked.

"Why?" she pleaded. "There's nothing left. What's the use?"

"I have to stay. That's all."

"They'll just burn that place too!"

"Will you?"

He looked at her. Her hair was tangled. Her eyes were still bloodshot from crying, and the hollows beneath them were dark from lack of sleep.

"Don't you know how scared I am?" she pleaded.

"Will you?" He stared at her until she raised her head and looked at him.

"What am I supposed to say, no? You know I will. Where would I go?"

He stood beside her and nodded, then threw a stone into the water, shattering the reflection of the fire.

When a grass fire had erupted, Ritter had permitted them to spray the open ground around the house, and finally, at dawn, he let them extinguish the smoking chars. The crowd left when the last wall had fallen and the house was nothing more than a heap of burning rubble. Then Fletcher, with Paxton, approached Ritter with a mimeographed form he had begun filling out inside one of the cabs. He asked Ritter if he knew how the fire had started.

Ritter snarled, "Don't waste my time!"

"What do you mean?"

"You know what I mean!"

"I don't."

"It was set! Burned! Call it what you want!" With a jerk of his arm he began to walk away.

"Can you prove that?" Fletcher asked.

"Prove it?" Ritter wheeled and glared at him. "Can you?"

"We might've," said Paxton, "if there'd been anything left."

"You might've!" Ritter snarled and spat. "You might've proved it was carelessness. Or maybe an overheated chimney. But not arson. You couldn't prove that. It would be beyond your *means* to prove that! Might have to build a jail around the whole town!" He paused and sighed.

"They didn't have electricity, did they? Used candles and lanterns?" Paxton waited for Ritter to answer, then turned to Fletcher. "That's your best bet."

"Get out of here!" Ritter ordered both of them. He walked away and ignored the roar of the last fire truck when it left.

Chapter Seventeen

It was a cool, gray morning. The dew had awakened those who had managed to sleep on the ground. They gathered their few possessions still strewn about the yard and prepared to leave. Ritter, Christine and Josh stood watching while the others piled quietly into the back of the hearse. They did not look at Ritter when they thanked him for all he had done; they seemed both stunned by what had happened and ashamed for giving up though they had not heard of Ritter's offer and did not know that they had any real choice. Some of them were bitter, especially Alice and Jerry, but they made no effort to express their feelings even to one another. Neither did they look at one another as they lay in the hearse with their legs intertwined and their heads on one another's laps.

Before the back door was closed, Jerry leaned out and drew a hex in the air in the direction of the valley.

"A curse on this town. May the hell that does not exist be made to house them and the heaven they have destroyed rise up to haunt them." He paused, evidently out of words, and looked at Josh.

"Are you sure you want to dwell in this land of Nod? We'll find a place in the Village, open up a communal pizza house or something."

Josh said that he was staying. Jerry raised his hands over him and Christine. "Then may an invisible barbed wire fence be drawn around you. So long!" Jerry took Josh's arm. Christine said goodbye to the others. Ritter simply stared until they were gone.

Christine and Josh followed Ritter to his farm. Ritter told Christine to wait in the car and nodded for Josh to follow him. He no longer hid his exhaustion as he crossed the yard; shuffling slowly and carefully, with his head bowed, he seemed afraid that the earth would give way beneath him. Josh waited at the doorway to the living room while Ritter took a shotgun from the glass cabinet. "You know how to use it? I guess you do." Josh nodded. Ritter handed it to him gently, as though entrusting him with a valuable heirloom, then took a box of shells from a drawer.

"You don't have to shoot anybody."

"I'm not going to."

"Just have it there and wave it around for people to see if there's any trouble. Fire a practice shot now and then when you hear a truck going by on the road. They'll hear it and word will get around. Can she shoot?"

"No."

"She willing to learn?"

"She wouldn't touch one."

"Doesn't matter."

Ritter told Josh to wait. He went into the kitchen,

then up the stairs, and finally returned with a box full of cooking utensils, blankets and old clothes.

"If you need anything else, tell me."

"Thanks."

"You're foreman now. Salary stays the same."

"We don't need that much."

"The same!" Ritter led him to the door then turned and confronted him. "Are you staying, or just staying for a while?"

"I'm staying."

"The girl?"

"She'll stay. I think she'll stay."

"Good. Anybody comes near that place, throw them off!" He held the screen door open then shouted after him, "You're foreman! Trail boss!" he snickered.

Christine, who had gotten out of the car to pet the ponies, glanced at the shotgun, then questioningly at Josh.

"I'm not going to use it," he explained.

"Then why have it?"

"Just in case."

"In case of *what?* Give it back, Josh. Please."

"I *can't.* He'll never sleep unless I have it."

"Please!" she pleaded. "I don't want to live like that!"

"Look, I'm not even going to load it. I'll put it away somewhere. All right?"

She didn't answer.

During the following weeks they painted and repaired the cabin and harvested and jarred enough vegetables to see them through the winter. Most of the crop, however, had not yet ripened. They did not know what they would do with it when it did. Christine suggested opening a roadside stand, but Josh was opposed to it. It would mean selling to the townspeople with whom he wanted no contact, and who probably would not trade with them anyway.

"We could sell to Fletcher," Christine suggested, "and he could sell them in his store."

"You know he won't do that! He won't even let us buy anything."

"He might, now. You haven't tried."

"I'm not going to."

"But it will all go to waste!"

"No, it won't. We'll do something."

More and more frequently, Josh would cut her off impatiently and refuse to resolve their disagreements. She felt alone with him. She always had, but it had been different before the fire. Then, when they had been walking together or sitting in the orchard, he had glanced up occasionally, from whatever blade of grass or weed that he was studying, and had smiled at her to let her know what he was thinking. He had always been imagining the future, though he would rarely admit it, and she had often been able, empathically, to imagine it with him. There seemed, now, to be no future. Though they had finally found sanctuary from the world in the secluded cabin, they had also withdrawn from it entirely, hidden from it, and Josh seemed to hold no expectation or desire that it would change.

While the commune had existed she had been unaware of how much she had depended upon the others for companionship. Now that they were gone, and now that Josh so rarely spoke or revealed himself, she missed them more than she had ever thought possible. During the evenings, when he would leave her briefly to stand on the porch or walk by himself through the orchard, she was overcome with a suffocating loneliness. It did not matter that she tried to hide it from him when he returned, for, caught up in his bitterness, he either could not or refused to notice.

She tried to keep busy. She began painting and sketching the mountains as the leaves began to change. She read paperback books bought during their infrequent trips to Simpsonville. She cooked, made curtains and decorated the house with dozens of flowers picked from the long row they had planted in the spring. One afternoon, in an effort to change his mood, she led him up to the field and they picked flowers together. She sat in the field and had him arrange purple zinnias in a crown upon her head. She planted flowers in his buttonholes and slipped one between his lips, fastened one to the zipper of her jeans in imitation of a fig leaf. But the source of his laughter seemed shallow, as if it were only for her.

"Do you really want me here? Really?" she asked.

He stared at her for a long time, then smiled shyly. "Yes. I think I'd die if you left. I really think I would."

She wanted him to want her, to make love to her suddenly, and anywhere, but his mind was always somewhere else and his eyes were nearly always cold.

He spent nearly a week building and painting Posted signs, nailing them to apple trees along the road, and in the woods along the perimeter of Ritter's land. Christine thought them both ugly and unnecessary but she made the stencils and helped Josh paint the letters.

The sun set noticeably earlier each day. Brilliant autumn colors spread like liquid and mingled on the mountains. The evenings were brisk. Josh built a fire each night and borrowed more blankets from Ritter. Christine imagined the impending winter in the cabin, as bleak as those Ritter had described, and wondered how they would survive. In some ways, however, she looked forward to it; there would be less work to do, and the snow and cold and the long winter nights in the cabin might help bring them closer together. Most of all, she hoped that the snow, by covering the charred foundation of the farmhouse, and the field, might help to cover the events of the summer.

Ritter, desperate for apple pickers, had contacted a major fruit and vegetable company which had offered a meagre price for his crop but had agreed to supply migrant workers from a labor pool it maintained. They arrived in mid-September in a surplus army bus that had been repainted bright green. They were, for the most part, families of Southern blacks who had come directly from the Connecticut River Valley, where they had spent the summer caring for and harvesting vast, flat fields lined with vegetables and tobacco. Most of them chose to spend at least half the year in the North in order to avoid the hot, humid summers of Georgia and Alabama and because the pay was better. They worked for the fruit and vegetable company year-round in one part of the country or another.

Their foreman, named Tifkin, was a genial, middle-aged white man. He was partially bald, had a fat, tanned face and a paunch that drove the waist of his khaki pants down to his abdomen. His tan was always accented by a clean, white shirt. Ritter introduced Tifkin to Josh and Christine. Tifkin smiled at Christine and shook Josh's hand amiably. He revealed no disfavor with Josh's appearance; being accustomed to dealing with a wide variety of people, he considered himself without prejudice. They led him to the orchards across from where the farm had stood, where he had groups and families erect prefabricated fiberglas huts and chemical outhouses. When this task was completed, they began picking apples, some singing and others eying Josh and Christine, who were also picking, with obvious distrust.

At the end of the day the box loads of apples were loaded onto a truck which left on the first of many hauls to Boston.

Josh and Christine decided to let the migrants have the unharvested vegetables. They told Tifkin, who, in turn, told the workers, who expressed only mild gratitude. Neither Josh nor Christine guessed that Tifkin intended to pocket the money that would be saved, money that was taken out of the migrant's wages.

Tifkin invited them to dinner each night. Families gathered together or mingled beneath apple trees to eat from tin plates and sip coffee or beer. They were curious as to how the farmhouse had burned. When Josh told them of the commune and the trouble they had had, and how the farmhouse had finally been destroyed, the workers conveyed sorrow but no particular surprise. The story, however, helped to break down the barrier of distrust, issued warmth and a certain understanding between them.

The presence of the migrants brightened Christine and brought about the first noticeable change in Josh. He enjoyed sitting beside a fire each night and talking to them. They were simple, easy-going people who equally enjoyed talking about the places they had been and the few outstanding experiences they had had during their interminable years in the fields. Gradually, when they began to feel that he was one of them, they made references about how difficult life was for them in the South.

They spoke of Florida, where they would go after harvesting several more orchards in New England. When Christine said she had never been there, they invited her and Josh to join them. Christine, only half jokingly, expressed her interest to Josh; he smiled and said nothing. Later, when they were alone, he told her that they were slaves. She wondered why the migrants had never thought of starting communes.

169

"How long would they last?" Josh asked. "As long as we did?"

Only late at night, when the prefabricated shacks stood grotesquely in the shadows of the apple trees, reflecting moonlight and firelight, did the migrant workers and their way of life appear tragic to Christine.

In ten days the orchards were picked and the migrants boarded the bus, carrying bags of vegetables they had picked under orders from Tifkin. They drove away, some waving, others appearing already to have forgotten Josh and Christine, who stood watching.

Viewed from the porch at sunset, Ritter's first orchard resembled the skeletal remains of an inhuman army, frozen in time and space, robed in charred, worm-eaten flesh. Yet, paradoxically, each tree conveyed a stark beauty, the dead equally to the few that still bore stunted red fruit. Josh dug holes and Christine planted seedlings in the rows between the old trees; they did not cut the dead trees down.

Josh had moved the salt lick to the center of the old orchard, in front of the house. The deer found it and began to frequent it each night. Most were does and fawns that were nearly grown, but the antlers of the few bucks moving across the small field on moonlit nights resembled branches and made it seem as though the trees had come to life. They were always cautiously jerking their heads to study the lamplight that came from the cabin and reflected in their eyes while they listened for footsteps and other human sounds. At first, they would run each time Christine or Josh passed a window and cast a shadow upon the field, but decided quickly, perhaps instinctively, that the inhabitants of the cabin posed no threat to them.

The deer brought about a further change in Josh. They seemed, Christine observed, to represent proof of something to him, perhaps that everything had not, after all, been destroyed. They were, as he had said, a free and invisible civilization, flourishing as if in ignorance of a world to which they no longer seemed to belong, yet always observant and acutely aware of the threat it posed to them.

Josh and Christine began to spend evenings on the porch watching them quietly, or talking about them when they were not there. Sitting in an old, wicker rocker that Ritter had given them, Josh would pull her into his lap and slide his hands into the slits between the buttonholes of the old overcoat she wore, then press them against her belly to keep them warm.

One evening they lay perfectly still in front of the cabin as a doe and fawn trotted out of the woods toward the salt lick. He waited until their heads were bowed over the salt, then rose slowly to a crouch. Each time the doe glanced up as though it had detected his movement, he would freeze. Finally, he stood with his hands at his sides. The doe, licking the salt from her lips, did not distinguish his human shape.

"Hello, deer," he whispered. The doe gave a start, glanced nervously at the fawn then back at Josh.

"Hello hello hello," he chanted softly, but made no move.

The doe and fawn cocked their heads, confused. Josh chanted again as he began taking slow, almost undetectable steps toward her. Suddenly, with a startling nod of her head, she fled. The fawn, paused for a moment, glancing between her and Josh, then ran after her, bounding behind her into the woods. Josh, smiling, turned to Christine.

171

"They weren't really afraid. They just knew they were supposed to be."

"What were you trying to do?"

"Touch them."

"Why?"

"I don't know," he shrugged. "I want to teach them not to be afraid. To get close enough to them to know what they're thinking."

She stood and walked toward him. They smiled at one another. Then he put his arms around her and rocked her back and forth, whispering that he was sorry.

When most of the leaves had fallen and the rest had lost their color, there was a week of Indian summer. With an abundance of free time, they spent most of these days walking through the woods, often trying to track and learn the habits of the deer. They would come upon as many as a dozen in a single afternoon. The animals, when caught by surprise, would sometimes return their gaze before stirring up layers of leaves as they fled. Josh and Christine would sit on mounds of moss that grew in clearings in pine woods. Josh would study patches of rich, black loam where the deer had pawed the moss and eaten it.

One small clearing about a quarter mile from the cabin became their favorite. It was completely locked in by pines, and boulders of quartz erupted from its moss and lichen-covered ground. One afternoon they lay there naked during the few hours when the sun was warm enough and not hidden behind the trees. They rolled in the lichen and covered their bodies with chalk designs. After they had made love, Josh lay with his head propped on his elbow and studied her.

"Do you believe in reincarnation?"

"Sometimes," she answered. "When I don't really think about it."

172

"What would you be next if you could choose?" he asked. "I know it's childish, but tell me anyway."

"I don't know."

"Come on! What would you be? A horse? A grasshopper? A mouse? A deer?"

Christine lay, smiling at him, with her face partially hidden behind her hair. "There's only one right answer, isn't there?" she asked.

"You'd be a deer," he told her. "Wouldn't you?"

"Okay."

"Sure you would. And I'd be a buck. And we'd wander around further north, maybe in Canada."

"Why there?"

"There are less people."

"In a herd?" she asked.

"Maybe," he smiled and paused to think about it. "Maybe we'd try that again. If we were deer."

"Josh, what are we going to do?"

"How do you mean?"

"Do you really want to stay here?"

"You don't?"

"Now, I do. I think I do. For a while I didn't think I could. Do you know?"

"Yes."

"But it doesn't seem as though it's something that can last, as though we can always live by ourselves. We're surrounded by people who hate us."

"It can last," he said simply.

"I suppose it can. But have you thought of trying anything else?"

"What?"

"We could join another commune. You wouldn't have to start it."

"No."

"Why?"

"I have to stay here. I don't know why."

"Do you think Ritter is going to will you the orchards?"

Josh rolled onto his side and stared at her. "Are you asking me if that's why I'm staying?"

"No."

"Maybe it is, partly. But I'd just as soon not think so. I'd just as soon not think about that now."

"I didn't mean it that way."

"I've been thinking about children," he said, abruptly changing the subject.

"How?"

"I thought we might have some if you wanted to? Would you?"

"I don't know. I'm afraid of them."

"They wouldn't be like the ones you're afraid of. They'd be anonymous, like Horace. We'd invite Alice up to deliver them. We'd hide them when the census people came around and teach them to live like the deer."

"Are you serious?"

"I don't know," he grinned.

They heard something moving in the woods. Expecting to see another deer, Josh walked, naked, to the edge of the clearing, held back the branches of a young pine tree and stared. Two hunters in camouflaged overalls noticed the movement of the branches, wheeled with bows and arrows and prepared to shoot. They stared, open-mouthed, then looked at one another and began laughing as Josh disappeared. They walked away whistling and snickering loudly enough so he could hear.

When they left the clearing the hunters were gone. They hurried uphill toward the cabin. Christine, frightened and holding Josh's hand, struggled to keep up with him.

Chapter Eighteen

At dawn they were awakened by rifle fire. Josh leaned, shirtless, against the porch rail. Christine stood behind the screen door, wrapped in her white fur robe, watching him as he listened and stared intently each time a shot was fired. Although many were merely pulsing sounds from miles away, others were piercing, crackling explosions that obviously emanated from within the perimeter of Ritter's property. They split the air and left a momentary vacuum of silence before another shot was fired.

Josh slid into a work shirt and tied back his hair. He took the shotgun from beneath the bed and began to load it.

"What are you going to do?"

"I'm going to walk the boundary and throw them off."

"You don't need that," she nodded toward the shotgun, remaining a safe distance both from it and him.

"They won't listen to me if I don't have it."

"Why does it have to be loaded?"

He didn't answer her or look at her. She met him at the door.

"Josh, what's the use? You can't be everywhere at once!" she pleaded. "You'll only wind up getting into fights!"

"I won't."

"Suppose they don't listen to you? A lot of those people would just as soon shoot you!"

"They're trespassing! That's all I'm going to tell them."

"Please don't go."

"I have to! I promised Ritter."

"You don't have to. You know that. It's what you want!" He started out the door. "I'll come with you," she said.

"No."

"I have to! I can't stay here!"

"No!" he shouted. "Stay in the house."

"Please! I can't stay here without you."

"I won't be gone that long."

"That's not what I mean! You know what I mean! I can't be alone here again."

He hesitated, then hurried down the stairs and did not look back at her.

The few full brown leaves that still clung to the apple trees fluttered and shivered in the wind. The bark of the trees was scaly and dark in the oblique, early morning, autumn light. Small crooked branches that had borne fruit weaved stark patterns against the clear sky or hung like the stems of willows toward the ground. About a dozen cars, half with out-of-state plates, were parked along either side of the road. Josh reached through the open window of the first car he approached, began beating the horn impatiently, then let it blare for a full minute. He waited and watched, but no one came to the road. He listened to the rifle fire, which had dwindled now that the deer had been warned, then walked up the hill toward the foundation of the old farm, turned and gazed over the orchard but saw no one. He strode into the woods in the direction of Ritter's farm.

"Nothing you can do about them once they're in the woods," Ritter explained. "Gotta get up earlier and catch them coming. There's no need to get so worked up."

"I don't want them around!"

"Neither do I, but it's easier said than done."

Ritter poured him a cup of coffee, then took three hard biscuits from the refrigerator and handed two to Josh. He nodded toward the kitchen table. They sat across from one another.

"You still got that salt lick?"

"Yes."

"A lot of deer?"

Josh nodded.

Ritter shook his head. "Not a very good idea to invite them around. They'll chew up those seedlings when the snow starts falling and they start getting hungry."

"I'll fence the trees."

Ritter broke a piece off one of the rolls and shoved it into his mouth. He sucked on it until it was soft enough to chew.

"Hunters aren't all a bad thing, you know. I don't like them because a lot of them come up from the cities and can't tell a deer from a horse, and I'm afraid they'll shoot one of the ponies. A deer rifle can put a good hole in an apple tree and open it up for disease. But deer are just as hard on the younger trees, and they'll tear down fences too when they put their minds to it." He paused and sipped his coffee, then glanced at Josh over the steaming cup. "I'm too old to aim a rifle, but you might get one yourself seeing as they're so handy. I'd pay you for the meat if you won't eat it. Venison's as good as steak."

"No."

"Suit yourself."

Josh rose to leave. He felt trapped in the old man's stare and suffocated by the scent of burnt coffee and old age, angered and frightened by the fact that he and Ritter were, suddenly, strangers.

"Do you want them kept off?"

"Yes!" Ritter snapped. "I'm just saying don't get carried away. The way you came in here with that rifle I thought something had happened. Everything else all right?"

"Yes."

"I talked to Fletcher the other day. He's willing to sell to you, as long as it's only you and the girl."

"I won't go in there again."

"Suit yourself." Ritter sucked the dry paste of roll from his gums. "Stop by in the morning before dawn. We'll catch them coming."

When Josh arrived back at the cabin Christine had gone. He glanced about the room, thinking that she was hiding from him, then walked onto the porch and called her. When he went inside again he found a note on the bed.

I have to go. If I waited and tried to explain I wouldn't be able to—I wouldn't be able to leave with you here. You've left me alone again and I'll go crazy here alone. And I'm scared of you even though I know it's wrong. But you've changed until

I don't know you and then I wonder if I ever did. I know that's wrong too, but you let them do this to you—it's as if you want to hate them and fight them even though you know it's no use. They'll burn the commune and kill the deer. Nothing you can do will stop them. There's nothing left here—can't you see? You have to let things go.

I'll write you from New York and ask you to come. If you don't, I don't know what I'll do. I love you.

He sped out of the orchard and down the mountain road, sure that she could not have gotten far, sure at each turn in the road that he would see her, with her head bowed and her long hair dangling, walking slowly, hoping that he would find her. By the time he reached . the town he was panic-stricken. He ran into the store. Fletcher, frightened, reached for something beneath the counter.

"I'm looking for the girl! The one who is always with me."

"She's gone."

"Where?"

"She got a ride into town about a half hour ago. Caught another one in front of the store a few minutes later." Fletcher eyed Josh suspiciously. "What'd you do to her?" Did you do something to her?"

"What kind of car?"

"You tell me first what you want her for."

"What kind of car?" Josh pleaded. "Please!"

"A yellow car. New York plates. That's all I know."

He drove perhaps thirty miles, through several small towns, passing dozens of cars until he saw a yellow sedan ahead of him as he came out of a curve. He swerved into the left lane on the first straight stretch of road, pulled up beside it and stared. The driver rolled down his window and cursed; the girl beside him frowned. Josh passed and did not look back at them. The road forked. He pulled off onto the shoulder and stopped, unable to decide which way to turn. Finally, his hands trembling, he lay his forehead against the wheel and closed his eyes.

He sat on the porch rail with his hands in his pockets, shivering in the cool, dry afternoon, listening to the occasional rifle shot that echoed up from the valley. There was no longer anything for his mind to take hold of, nothing around which his thoughts could revolve except his sudden, irrational fear of the night he would spend alone. He couldn't go inside the cabin. Everything about it was as alien to him as if he had never lived there; it was difficult even to remember where he was. He hated her for leaving him as much as he needed her. He was drawn to the part of himself that she contained and it seemed that this magnetism was trying to lead him away from the orchards to his death; for his life was somehow tied inextricably to the orchards, as though to give up and leave them would be to walk off the face of the earth.

A doe hobbled out of the woods with a deep, ugly gash in her thigh. The bone had been shattered, and her leg dangled like a chestnut sack as she limped across the field. Rivulets of blood ran beneath her belly and down her leg. Leaves and twigs were stuck to the wound from the times that she had fallen. She stopped, dazed, shook her head in pain and gazed about the orchard, then limped instinctively toward the salt lick. She bent over the salt lick and tried to lick it, as though her shock and loss of blood had made her forget that she was dying.

Seized with pain, she shook her head again, then fell and tried to roll as if she thought she could rub the wound off upon the ground. She tried to rise and found that she could not, kicked and writhed momentarily, then lay quietly, panting.

She saw him walking toward her but was paralyzed by the pain, weakened from her loss of blood and no longer had the will to try to stand or run. When he stood above her, her small black eyes stared up at him, seemed to recognize him, to be pleading with him or trying desperately to ask him a question. She flinched as he raised the shotgun. He closed his eyes and fired, exploding her head.

He turned away without looking at what he had done and saw Henry and his brother approaching the edge of the woods.

"There it is!" Henry shouted. "Hey! Was that doe hit in the hip before you got her?"

"Get out of here," Josh said quietly. The two boys stopped at the field.

"Was she hit or not?" Henry asked angrily. "If she was, she's mine!"

"Get out of here!"

"That's the one," said Cal. "I know it is."

"Listen! That doe's mine. The law says so, that it's mine if I get it first no matter whose land it winds up on."

"Besides, this ain't your land!" Cal added.

Josh raised the shotgun and aimed it at Henry.

"Get out of here!"

"You can't! You can't do that! It's against the law!"

Josh fired. The blast struck Henry directly in the face. His head, reeling backwards, seemed to lift his body off the ground. Cal staggered from his shock at the blast. He tripped and fell, screamed as he saw his brother's body, crawled, then ran screaming into the woods.

Ritter, sitting on the front porch in his overcoat, heard shouting, glanced up, squinted and saw what appeared to be someone running down the road waving a stick. He shuffled toward the road certain that there had been a hunting accident, having seen at least a half dozen during his life. He feared for a moment that it was Josh, then discerned that the figure was too small and stout.

Tears streamed down Cal's face. He sobbed and gasped for breath, staring wildly at Ritter, then moaned that someone had been killed.

"Who?"

"Henry! He's dead! I know he is!"

"Where?"

"The cabin! He murdered him! He just—" Cal moaned and covered his face with his hands as though it were he who had been shot. Then he lurched forward and vomited on the road and down the front of his red hunting jacket. Ritter's body fell and rose with each deep, uneven breath. He stared blankly at his feet. His knees weakened; it seemed to him that his body was being sucked into the earth. He closed his eyes and fought with all his strength to stand. Then he heard Cal running toward the house.

"Where are you going?"

"Police!"

"I haven't got a phone."

Cal's eyes darted between the house and the road. He saw Ritter's truck, ran for it and lept into the cab. Ritter watched it swing out of the driveway toward town. When the truck was out of sight he shuffled after it with his frail arms dangling at his sides.

182

He walked down the path and through the narrow boundary of woods that separated the old orchard. He walked into the orchard without calling Josh or giving him any warning. He climbed the porch steps and opened the cabin door. The rifle lay by the kitchen sink. Water in the aluminum wash basin was pink. Josh had gone.

He found blood on a trail of matted grass and followed it to the woods. A few feet inside the woods, surrounded by brown and brightly colored leaves, the carrion of the doe was stacked atop Henry. Entrails and shattered bone were all that remained of the doe's head. Henry, faceless, lay on his back with his arms outspread. His forehead and part of his skull had been blown away, and his blood mingled with the fallen leaves. Beside them lay a shovel, and near it a small hole where the digging of a grave had been quickly interrupted by rocks and roots. Ritter began to wheeze. He rubbed his wrinkled forehead and turned dumbly away.

He sat on the porch steps gathering his breath until he heard them closing in on the orchard through the woods. Hunters who had been gathering outside Fletcher's store in the late afternoon to drink beer and tell stories had waited with Cal for the police and followed them up the mountain. Several of them, along with troopers and deputies, surrounded the old orchard. Paxton crouched behind a tree near the entrance and saw Ritter.

"Ritter! Tell him to come out!"

Ritter stood and shuffled toward him.

"Get out of the way!" Paxton shouted.

Ritter stopped in front of him and stared. "He's gone."

Paxton stood. Suddenly, from the other side of the orchard someone fired at the cabin. Then there was a series of explosions as the hunters and less-disciplined police opened fire. Every window in the cabin was shattered. Paxton screamed at them to stop. He glanced over his shoulder at Ritter who was walking up the path.

"Stay here!"

Ritter either ignored him or did not hear. He trudged up the path bent forward with his hands in the pockets of his overcoat. He found his truck in the road, its engine running, climbed into it and drove home.

The two ponies were hovering near the barn, swishing their tails and shaking their heads anxiously as though they sensed that something was wrong. They watched Ritter enter the house.

He sat slumped over the kitchen table rubbing his eyes, nodding involuntarily. Then he heard a movement in the living room and what resembled the sound of a match striking against stone. He listened as the blowing, crackling noise of fire became more clear. His heart raced until his chest was pierced by a sharp, burning pain. He stood, dizzy with dread, and walked slowly to the doorway of the living room.

Josh, kneeling beside the fireplace, glanced up at him. They stared at one another for several moments, then Ritter, clenching his fists to keep his hands from shaking, shuffled closer to him. When the old man stood above him Josh turned and stared intently at the fire.

"I'm going to try to get away."

Ritter paused, pressed his lips together and nodded.

"Then you'd better go. They're after you right now."

"I had to see you first."

"You don't have time."

"I won't be able to see anybody I know again. I thought of that and I had to stop. You know?"

Josh's eyes darted up at Ritter, then back at the fire. The paper he had used to light it had disintegrated. The dry, split apple logs stacked in a pyramid had begun burning with a steady orange flame. Ritter collapsed into an easy chair and gripped its tattered arms.

"I warned him."

"Warning is legal. Killing isn't."

"Isn't it?" He looked squarely at Ritter. The old man met his eyes.

"No."

Josh stood and slid his hands into his hip pockets.

"I took some of your food. Do you mind?" He nodded toward a paper bag on the floor.

"No."

"I'm going to try not to run. If I go into the woods and keep walking maybe they won't find me."

"Maybe," Ritter muttered.

"This will cause you trouble. I'm sorry."

"That's not the thing to be sorry for."

"I'm not sorry for killing him. I keep telling myself I'm supposed to be, but it doesn't make any difference. It's like I'm not here—like I'm somewhere else watching myself. Do you know?"

Ritter shook his head and could no longer look at him, frightened by what he saw in Josh's eyes. Josh picked the bag off the floor.

"I'd better go."

"Wait!"

Ritter forced himself out of the chair and crossed to a bureau. The top drawer wedged as he tried to open it. He yanked at it violently, then took out a pair of scissors.

"Cut your hair. That's what they'll be looking for."

Josh grabbed his hair where it was gathered and hacked at it until the knot came off in his hand. He threw it into the fire. It sizzled, then burst into flames emitting the sickening odor of burning flesh.

"I'm not going to watch which way you go. I don't want to know."

"Thanks."

"Don't!" Ritter snapped.

They nodded at one another. Ritter stared at him intently as though to wish him luck although he could not say it. Josh walked quickly over the meadow toward the woods. The ponies followed him.

Minutes later Paxton and two other police officers beat upon Ritter's door, then opened it when he did not answer. When they asked if they could search the house he nodded, then sat motionless in front of the fire and did not acknowledge them further as they went through each room with their pistols drawn. When they left, he did not bother to glance up at them.

Ritter watched the fire settle and gradually crumble to pulsing orange coals. He watched the coals grow white until only a trickle of smoke spun up the chimney. He listened to dozens of patrol cars and carloads of hunters race past his house. He listened also to intermittent rifle shots, not knowing whether they were firing at the deer or Josh.

He wondered whether he, too, was insane. Then it occurred to him that it didn't matter. It occurred to him that he could no longer care for anything and that he would have to die even sooner than he had planned.